TARTH
Book Two

UNDER THE GOLDEN MISTS

S.G. BYRD

OAKTARA

WATERFORD, VIRGINIA

Under the Golden Mists

OakTara Publishers
P.O. Box 8
Waterford, VA 20197

Visit OakTara at
www.oaktara.com

Cover design by David LaPlaca/debest design co.
Cover image, © iStockphoto/Aimin Tang
Author photo © 2009 by Mike Stepp

ISBN: 978-1-60290-095-0

♯ ♯ ♯

To all those who don't know
what gift God has given them
and who sometimes wonder
if they even have one.

Acknowledgments

Many writers say, "I could not have written this book without the support of my family"—with good reason. It's true. Christian writers will often add to that, "God gave me ideas and pushed/led/nudged/kicked when I needed it." That's also true. Many thanks to my family and my God!

We have a cabin between West Jefferson and Todd, North Carolina, in what I consider the most beautiful mountains in the world, the Blue Ridge Mountains. For years, en route to our cabin, we'd travel out of our way to get cinnamon buns at The Three Bears Restaurant, located next to The Greenhouse Crafts Shop in Glendale Springs. My mouth would start watering a hundred miles away for Randy and Helen Baldwin's cinnamon buns! As Lacht says, "The cinnamon and sugar and butter ran together the way I like them to, and the bread part was good enough to enjoy all by itself!" Thank you, Randy and Helen, for sharing your recipe.

I want to thank these proofreaders and supportive friends from Church of the Good Shepherd in Durham, NC—in alphabetical order, Karen Bohn; Lee Bowen; David and Andriani Carson; Liz Heinmiller; Martha Hopper; Pat Kiefer; Gwillim Law; Julie, Nathan, and Colleen McKeel; Elizabeth Monk; Sheila Parry; Mike and Gail Stepp; Lynn Trogdon; Connie Walker; and Bonnie Whitney.

Also heartfelt thanks to the publishing staff of Oaktara. Jeff sought me out; Ramona gave me helpful editing and steady encouragement; and David, the designer of *Under the Golden Mists'* cover, thrilled me with my first glimpse of a Tarth landscape.

One

The Stalli Guide

Tarth's Root Forest had more than its share of roots, and though some of them grew underground, enough erupted above the forest floor to make walking difficult. Lacht didn't care. She didn't want to leave.

She grimaced to keep from crying, not that anyone in her group would have noticed. They'd all turned their backs to her, but that didn't mean she wanted to move away from them.

"So you see," she told the gray hair curling down five young teenagers' backs, "Keshua wants us to love each other."

The girls and boys, peering through gaps in the roots around them, didn't respond.

They wanted to see the guide from Stalli who had arrived late last night to take Lacht's family away. The Stalli family who had lived so long in the Root Forest looked strange—everyone knew that—but did all Stallis look that way, or was it only their friends?

Lacht rolled her eyes and thought about scolding them. After all, she was eighteen years old now, a young woman and the leader of the group; however, if she stayed quiet and stepped to the left, she could see through an unoccupied gap.

One step and the gap was claimed, but she did start counting inside her mind.

One, two...forty-six, forty-seven, forty....

"Oh, Lacht," asked Softbark finally in the Root people's guttural language, "are you done?"

"Ye-e-e-s," Lacht drawled the Root word out slowly, with a trace of sternness.

Softbark was one of her favorite Root girls, but she thought the group should know they had not paid proper attention.

"Good," commented Graybark, Softbark's younger brother, without turning. "You were distracting me."

Lacht shook her head at Graybark's back, but a smile almost formed on the corners of her lips—almost, but not quite.

Soggy faces did not smile, and she had cried so much over the last two weeks that not only her face, but part of her neck felt waterlogged.

Early that morning, she'd slipped out of the family root cave, deliberately escaping the last day of packing. She'd done her share of the work up until then, but someone else could carry the heavy bags to the forest edge.

That Stalli guide could carry them.

She had not wanted to meet the man on her last morning in the Root Forest. She'd known she wouldn't like him.

Why was she spying on him anyway?

"I think I should go home," she said, but just then Mosslimb waved a big hand right in her face.

"He is here!"

Root people didn't get excited often, but when they did, their excitement spread as quickly as moss on the damp forest floor. Lacht peered through her gap and saw her stepfather walking with a young man toward their cave.

Winnel always kept his hair long enough to tie back with a string because, he'd announced many times, he could cut the whole thing with two or three snips of the scissors. Gray hairs had begun mingling with the darker ones now, but Lacht didn't give Winnel more than a cursory glance, not with the guide from Stalli walking right next to him.

The young man had his back to her, but that didn't hide his broad shoulders. All Stallis had either black or dark brown hair, but this man's black hair, trimmed evenly about his ears, was unusually thick. When he turned her way, she caught her breath and grabbed hold of the nearest root.

She'd never seen a more attractive man.

The Root teens cast sideways glances at each other. Several of them shrugged.

"He is probably nice," commented Softbark kindly.

"Is he a grownup?" asked Graybark. "What happened to him?"

"Shhh," cautioned Mosslimb. "They must all be like that."

Root Forest people never cut their gray curly hair. Both men and women wore it long down their backs, but it wasn't the newcomer's short black hair that had prompted the group's negative reaction. Root people had adjusted to Stalli hair years ago.

"Berries like berries," Lacht remarked casually.

She knew exactly what had caused the sideways glances and shrugs. Her friends still could not understand why Stallis had such weak little hands and feet. Stalli heads were small too.

"Plums like plums," she continued in the same relaxed voice.

The Root teenagers cocked their big heads to one side and stared at her.

"I do not think that is true," Graybark said. "We like berries and plums, but they do not like each other. How can they? They are not alive!"

Usually, she explained herself with great patience to her friends. Tonight, she didn't want to take the time.

"I'll see you tomorrow," she said, swinging herself between two roots and sliding down another.

"Berries do not like plums either," one of the girls whispered behind her. "They do not like anything at all."

That made a smile quirk again on the corners of Lacht's mouth, as she approached the roots that formed her home. The men had already gone in, and she brushed quickly past the vine entrance.

Irsht must have run away from the last day of packing too, because Winnel had just finished introducing her to the Stalli guide. Lacht had never seen her sister's eyes open that wide, almost Root-people wide. Irsht wasn't asking questions either, which indicated shock of no mean proportions.

Raising her chin an inch, the older girl braced herself not to show the same reaction. They'd only visited Stalli once, years ago. She and Irsht hadn't seen many Stalli men, that was all.

"Here's my older daughter," said Winnel, turning to put an arm around her shoulder. "Crispin, I'd like you to meet Lacht."

Crispin's eyes lit up and he smiled, showing unusually straight teeth that added to his attractiveness. Most Stalli teeth grew slightly crooked. Some grew greatly crooked, and Frenne had taught her girls to thank the Great One for their own straight teeth.

Quit thinking about teeth!

"Winnel, I will enjoy taking your family across the desert," the young man in front of Lacht stated, one of his hands making an elaborate half-circle in the air. "Everyone in the Stalli Mountain Range will applaud me, I am sure, for bringing two such lovely girls to our country!"

The sisters glanced at each other, and Lacht knew that Irsht didn't know what to say any more than she did. They'd never received compliments on their appearance. Root people felt sorry for them, even the ones who loved them; and Winnel and Frenne never spoke about a person's looks.

Frenne saved the situation by calling them to supper. Even in the midst of her confused feelings, Lacht nodded appreciatively at the table as she sat in her chair. She enjoyed color.

Mallowberry juice mixed with strawberry cider turned the glasses in front of each plate a bright red-orange. A blue vegetable casserole sat at one end of the table, while a platter full of the fried pinkplant fritters Irsht and Lacht always requested sat at the other. In the middle, yellowbud potatoes, mashed and buttered, flanked a beautifully browned turkey.

Someone must have given them the turkey. Frenne could hunt quite well, but she rarely wanted to take the time; and she had certainly not taken it on their last day of packing. Lacht had expected the normal melvefish, caught in the family fish trap.

No melvefish tonight, she thought, feeling her mouth water as she sniffed the aroma of roasted turkey.

"What's this?" asked Crispin, putting a fritter on his plate. "It smells delicious, but I don't think I've ever had it."

"Root people call it pinkplant," Frenne answered.

"Umm, pinkplant tastes as good as it smells," he announced after the first mouthful, "although I'm sure the cook knew exactly how to create such a wonderful flavor."

"Thank you," Frenne responded demurely enough, but Lacht saw the glitter of amusement in her mother's eyes.

The eighteen-year-old shifted in her chair, her thoughts jumping unexpectedly to their guest's defense. *What's wrong with complimenting people? It's just a form of encouragement! We should do it more often ourselves.*

Irsht had recovered from her uncharacteristic shyness. "Will you tell us about Stalli?" she asked their guest. "We visited a long time ago, but I don't remember much."

"Stalli is the most beautiful country on Tarth," Crispin announced with another hand flourish.

"I'm sure the Muntas and Paigens would disagree with you," Winnel commented.

"As would our own Root people," Frenne added. The glitter of amusement had spread from Frenne's eyes to her cheeks now, displaying both dimples.

Nothing daunted, Crispin countered, "Yes, but we have more mountains than they do—Stalli is all mountains! Our northern ranges spear the clouds. Snow covers their peaks even in the summer, while winter brings a frenzy of wild blizzards and below-zero temperatures."

Irsht's eyes had expanded to Root-people size again, and he smiled at her.

"Don't worry, little maiden; Stallis live in the southern mountains, where we welcome both the green of winter snows and the blue of summer leaves. The richest blue grass on Tarth abounds in Stalli's southern ranges. Our horses thrive on it."

He had lost her.

"I am not a little maiden!" Irscht stated, a pucker taking over her lips. "I'm almost sixteen!"

"My pardon," he responded promptly and bowed his head in acknowledgment of his error.

She nodded forgiveness, and Frenne urged her youngest daughter to pass the mashed potatoes and gravy to Winnel.

During that brief interval, Crispin glanced at Lacht and winked. Lacht almost laughed out loud but stopped herself in time. She didn't want to hurt Irsht's feelings—but a heady feeling rushed over her, and she didn't know what to do with her hands.

Their guide served himself a second helping of the mashed potatoes when the bowl came his way, covered the potatoes with gravy, and then leaned back in his chair. "Our wise ones received your letter from the Munta travelers and sent me to escort you to our village, situated on the shores of the most beautiful lake in Tarth. I must warn you, however. The water of our lake becomes green only when boiled. All other Stalli lakes are the normal green, but our lake is gold with golden mists that rise daily above its surface."

"Why is it different?" asked Irsht, almost before he had finished his last sentence.

"No one knows. At least, no Stalli know. Perhaps the inhabitants under the lake could tell us, but no one has heard from them for many years—not until two weeks ago, the day before I left to cross the desert."

"You've heard from the Wassandra?" blurted out Frenne, her eyebrows shooting to the middle of her forehead.

Crispin's eyebrows mirrored his hostess's. "You know about the Wassandra?"

She nodded, partially recovering from the surprise his words had given her. "My grandmother grew up in your Stalli village. That's one of the reasons we want to live there...that and the fact that Burkin Village needs a rope maker. My grandmother often

6

spoke of the mysterious Wassandra of Wasso Lake, but she'd never seen one of them."

"No communication has existed between us for three generations," he agreed.

Irsht broke into their conversation. "Wait a minute. Back up, please. Who are the Wassandra? How could they live under a lake—and if nobody has seen them, how do you know they're there?"

Everyone smiled at the fifteen-year-old's matter-of-fact attitude.

Her mother answered. "Let me, Crispin. We haven't given you time to eat."

Lacht lifted one eyebrow, then lowered it quickly before anyone could see her involuntary response. The young man had seconds on his plate of everything, plus a large serving of blueberry cobbler waiting in a side bowl. Nevertheless, good manners meant not making a guest do all the talking.

Frenne was a stickler for good manners.

"Stallis settled Burkin Village on the shores of Wasso Lake over two hundred years ago," she told her girls. "At first, the Wassandra came out of their lake and made friends. They could visit with other people, because they breathed air as easily as they breathed water."

"Nobody breathes water," objected Irsht immediately. She had quit eating so she could process this information. Irsht loved to learn new things.

"Well, I don't know what they do, then," amended Frenne, "but they live under the surface of the lake. The water doesn't buoy them up as it does us. They can walk or run through the lake as if it were dry land—or so I've heard. We Stallis have become ignorant over the years."

Crispin had demolished his food by this time. He pushed back from the table and raised one hand in what the family already recognized as a habitual gesture. "Our ignorance may have come to an end," he informed them with relish.

Obviously, he was one of those people who enjoyed telling news. Lacht kept her mouth tightly closed. Her lips wanted to open with excitement, and, if they opened, she felt unsure about her breathing.

Act your age!

"The day before I left to cross the desert, someone lifted the flag on the old message box," the young man announced.

Frenne gasped and Irsht opened her mouth, but Crispin answered the obvious question before she had time to ask it.

"When their friendship began to deteriorate, our ancestors built a pier and hung a small, water-resistant box at its end. Stallis and Wassandra left messages in the box instead of visiting, but even that custom died out over time. You can imagine how we felt when we saw the flag upright again."

He paused for dramatic effect, and Lacht had to restrain herself again from laughing out loud. Irsht knew no restraint.

"What did the message say?" she demanded impatiently.

"They've lost one of their children!" their guide announced.

Winnel jumped out of his chair. "Lost one of their children— how terrible!" he said, groaning as if the missing child belonged to him.

Lacht's eyes softened.

Neither she nor Irsht ever thought of Winnel as their stepfather. He'd loved them as daughters from the day he and Frenne married; and he loved the peoples of Tarth in much the same way, never concentrating on the differences between them, only on what they had in common.

"They asked if we had seen the child, an eleven-year-old girl," Crispin continued. "No one had, of course, and our wise ones placed a reply in the message box. They wouldn't let us on the pier, but my friends and I kept watch from the shore. The hours became tedious, but when the Wassandra finally returned, we were glad we had waited."

"Poor parents," Winnel spoke again, still standing beside his chair, but the girls didn't want to think about the poor parents just then.

"What did they look like?" they asked at the same time.

"Well," Crispin murmured, "they didn't come completely out of the water, which is, I might add, fourteen feet deep at the end of the pier. A pale arm reached from the water to the box and opened it with fingers that appeared to be longer than our fingers. That was all we saw, but it was enough! Burkin Villagers have begun keeping their children away from the lake's edge, especially at night when the mists creep up the shore."

Lacht and Irsht stared wide-eyed at him, but Winnel sat down abruptly, his face held in place as if he were keeping himself from frowning by deliberate willpower.

"Keshua created all peoples on Tarth," he insisted. "We must not judge the Wassandra by their appearance."

Lacht changed positions in her chair again. She agreed with her father in theory, but he needn't sound so rigid. "How exciting!" she said hurriedly.

"Yes, it was," Crispin agreed with her, "and who can say what we'll find when we return?"

"Is there an empty cottage in Burkin Village?" questioned Frenne, and the conversation shifted toward their move and new home.

Later that night, as the sisters prepared for bed in their small bedroom, they talked about the story Crispin had told them.

"An underwater people, of all things!" Irsht remarked happily.

"Where did that eleven-year-old girl go?" wondered Lacht. "She couldn't have come out of the lake. Someone would have seen her and reacted."

"I'd say!" agreed Irsht. "You would've heard my reaction all the way back to the Root Forest."

Lacht started to say something about not responding

negatively to people because they looked different, but she closed her lips tightly. She didn't want to sound like Winnel.

"Well, they'll probably find her before we get there," she said instead.

Irsht's face fell. "Do you think so?" she asked with evident disappointment.

"It'll take two weeks," Lacht reminded her. "If we didn't live on this side of the Root Forest, it would take longer."

"Yes, yes," the younger girl responded, yawning, "but still, I want to see that golden lake; don't you?"

"Umm hmm," Lacht answered absently.

The move didn't upset her as much now that she'd decided to like their guide. Lacht rolled her eyes at herself; nevertheless, she went to sleep with a happy anticipation that did not account for her dream....

In the middle of the night, long, vague things without a discernible color began waving in front of her, behind her, on both sides of her, and even above her. She stood in the middle of the wavy things, while fear threw itself at her mind.

Then she heard a voice. "Help me. Please, help me," it sobbed. "Help me—," but with the repeated cry, Lacht sat up in bed, breathing heavily, and clutched the covers.

It was a bad dream, she told herself. *Only a bad dream!*

Two

The Desert

The next morning, Lacht couldn't have cared less about Crispin or any other Stalli for that matter. Her heart felt soggy now—and heavy.

"Do you remember playing hide 'n' seek there?" she asked Mosslimb as she pointed toward some particularly jumbled roots.

"Yes," Mosslimb answered and added, "Why do you have to go, Lacht?"

"Mom and Dad want to," she answered, voice catching.

Why do we have to go?

Irsht marched purposefully past with her arms over the shoulders of her two closest Root Forest friends, the three of them headed in the direction of the nearest blueberry patch for one last mouth-staining visit.

Lacht sighed. Her friends had come individually to tell her good-bye. As each of them had left, disappearing into the shadowed depths of the Root Forest, a part of her had left too. Very little remained by this time—only sore eyes and a soggy heart that dragged four feet behind her everywhere she went.

They did not plan to return to the Root Forest. Letters would have to do.

"We need to make a new home," Frenne had explained. "We need to look forward; not backward."

Her older daughter didn't understand.

Twelve years ago, after helping win the war against the evil sorcerer, Gefcla, Winnel and Frenne had moved to the forest so they could tell the Root people about Keshua. When the Great One had brought his Son back to life, he'd promised to give anybody who loved him life too, life that would never end; they had doggedly insisted throughout those early years of resistance and hostility.

Lacht could remember a time when Root mothers called their children away from playing with her and Irsht. Slowly, over the years, the situation had changed; now they had many friends, and a large number of the Forest people met regularly to stomp their feet and sing their joy.

Did Frenne and Winnel think no one needed them anymore?

"That's ridiculous," she muttered. "Mom and Dad are leaders. People always need leaders."

"We're almost ready," called her mother.

Dragging a heavy heart after her, Lacht walked to where Frenne and Winnel stood visiting with a small group of Root people.

"You said you had come to stay!" snarled one of the men.

Lacht recognized that voice. *Mudde.* The Root man always made trouble. He had fought in Gefcla's army many years ago and been badly disappointed when his dreams of domination had failed.

For twelve years, Winnel had tried to make friends with him, but the old warrior had consistently ignored him whenever he talked about Keshua. Mudde had finally accepted Winnel himself, after a fashion. He'd just had no use for Keshua.

"Twelve years," one of the other men said slowly. "They have lived with us for twelve years."

Mudde's lips puckered as if he'd taken a bite of sourplum, and Winnel tried to explain.

"Our daughters have never known their own land or people. Soon they will want to marry and have families of their own. We are going back to Stalli for them."

The Root people, all except for Mudde, nodded.

12

Without making any noise, Lacht slipped away, her heart pounding and her thoughts clamoring—so that was why her parents had decided to leave.

"And all this time, I thought they wanted to go," she said out loud.

"We do," responded Frenne from behind her.

Obviously, her mother had seen her slip away and followed.

"But your work—" Lacht argued.

"We've done what the Plete told us to do here," Frenne told her evenly. "Now he is directing us to Stalli. Both of us feel the new guidance—and we must obey."

Lacht nodded automatically.

"In many ways, we're happy to return," the older woman continued with a smile, though her eyes were red.

Had her mother cried last night?

"We'll find people to love in the Stalli Mountains too, you know." Lacht jerked out another nod, and Frenne patted her on the back. "It's time to go," she said quietly. "Where's Irsht?"

"Blueberries," Lacht answered briefly.

Her mother laughed. "I should have known." She moved off to find her younger daughter, blue-stained mouth and all.

The family left, walking through the deeply shaded Root Forest for the last time. Lacht's heart dragged along the path behind them, and her feet wanted to run back to join it, but she wouldn't let them.

Crispin would have finished loading the horses by now. The Stalli Mountain horses had willingly crossed the desert to help with the move, but they wouldn't want to wait, not with heavy bags on their backs.

As her family walked through the speckled shade of the last few trees, she noted suddenly the small number of Root people who walked with them.

Didn't they have more friends than that?

By the time she stepped out of the forest onto the red sands of the desert, Lacht was stomping almost as hard as a Root man could stomp. The brilliance of the desert sun made her eyes water, but she didn't squint. She was too angry to squint.

Her mother and father had spent twelve years of their lives working with these people. *You'd think—*

Singing startled her, and she spun around in the sand.

On the border of the forest, stretching in either direction as far as she could see, a line of people stood in the last of the shade. Big feet stomped, keeping time to the song; and oversized hands lifted partly in worship of Keshua and partly to block out the bright sunlight that reflected from the sand only a few feet away.

Their large eyes wincing in pain, the people sang to Keshua in honor of the couple who had chosen to live with them for twelve years. Lacht had never heard of Root men and women voluntarily coming this close to the desert glare.

Gefcla had forced his army to march across the sand one summer's day twelve years ago. She'd heard about that, of course; but she knew that the army had gone only because they feared Gefcla more than exposure to the sun.

Fear was not what had brought Root people to the desert today.

Her parents stopped and turned. Holding hands, they sang along with their friends. When the song ended, Winnel lifted his hands and asked the Great One to bless them all, those staying and those leaving.

Lacht stared down the long line of Root Forest people until she spotted Softbark waving. With a rush, she ran to her friend and hugged her one last time. "I can't stand to go," she moaned.

"You must find your berry," Softbark told her kindly.

"Or your plum," Graybark added from behind his sister. "I like plums better," he commented helpfully.

Lacht smiled. Though slow to grasp a new idea, the Root

people never forgot something once they understood it.

"Lacht," called her mother.

"Let's go," shouted Crispin at the same time.

It was when they had mounted and begun to move away, that the unbelievable happened. Someone yelled gruffly from the forest edge, too gruffly for Lacht to understand the words.

Then she saw Mudde moving out from under the protection of the trees into the bright sunlight. Sour-faced Mudde, looking singularly sour even for him, ran across the desert sands toward Winnel, who bent to grasp the Root Forest man's big hands.

Lacht couldn't hear what Mudde said, but his words made Winnel's face glow.

Mudde didn't stay long. He finished what he had to say and bolted back to the shelter of the trees, as if his bushy gray curls might catch on fire if they stayed another second in the sun. Winnel turned, lifted his hands again, and called out one more blessing.

Then they left. Her father's eyes streamed for over an hour with more tears than the brightness of the desert could have caused.

♫ ♫ ♫

By the end of the first week, Lacht was no longer sad. It was embarrassing, really embarrassing, but she couldn't make herself feel sad even when she tried.

They'd met a small group of Muntas heading toward Stalli the third day out, and the two groups had joined to form one large group. Timidogs posed the only threat on the desert these days, and the sly, desert dogs never attacked large groups of travelers.

Nevertheless, when long, drawn-out wails quavered through the desert air, she shivered. She shivered and enjoyed doing so, though she would never have admitted it out loud.

Irsht had no such qualms. The younger girl dropped her

empty plate on top of her mother's one evening and boldly announced that she liked the eerie sound, especially when everyone sat around the fire, sipping hot mallowberry juice and telling the story of Lynn and the brueggen stones.

Irsht tilted her face and smiled suggestively as she raised the cup Frenne had just handed her. Her parents laughed, and one of the Munta men obligingly started the familiar story.

Lacht hugged her knees up to her chest and listened as if she'd never heard the tale before; though, at the end, she made the same comments she always made. "I don't understand how such an ordinary woman could've saved Tarth, even if she did come from another world. I mean, Lynn has three sons," she pointed out as if that fact alone erased all possibility of heroism. "She handles the business part of Chell's rock quarry. When we visited years ago, I saw her checking their fish trap—and cooking what she caught!"

"I agree," Irsht stated, backing her sister up with an opinionated nod. "She's too normal!"

"Don't forget Keshua," Winnel responded as he always did. "Without him, Lynn would have never seen Tarth, much less reached Shagger's Rock with two brueggen stones."

"We know, we know," the two girls droned, and Winnel raised an eyebrow at them.

"Well, we do know," Irsht said again, smiling pertly at her father.

Late in the afternoon of the next day, a call came from the riders in front of Lacht. She waved, then tightened her legs. Obligingly, her mare moved into a faster pace, and they soon caught up with Irsht and one of the Munta girls.

"We're over halfway there," Irsht announced.

"How do you know?" Lacht questioned, glancing around at the bright red sand. It held no discernible landmarks she could see.

"Crispin told us," her sister informed her. "He said we're making better time traveling with the Muntas, because they're in a hurry."

Lacht glanced around again.

"He's not here anymore," Irsht said with a knowing smirk. "You can stop acting silly."

"I am not acting silly," Lacht whispered furiously.

"You would be if Crispin was here," Irsht replied, still smirking; then the two younger girls galloped back to make their announcement to the rest of the group.

Lacht brushed red desert dust off her sleeves and tried to brush the irritation out of her feelings at the same time. She did not act silly around Crispin. What a ridiculously childish notion!

"Hello," said a deep voice, making her start.

"Oh, Crispin, I didn't see you coming," she said, blushing in a way she was glad Irsht couldn't see.

They rode together in a companionable silence. Low on the horizon, the sun shone with a mellow spirit. The air cooled several degrees, and the wind died down. Then, suddenly, everything went pink.

Lacht gasped with pleasure. No matter how many times she saw them, desert sunsets always thrilled her. The sky turned pink, the sands turned pink, and Crispin turned pink too, she noticed, when she glanced his way.

"You're pink," she told him, laughing out loud.

"Hard to avoid," he responded with a wink.

Smiling briefly, Lacht faced the front of her horse. She never knew what to do when the young man winked at her. *That's why he does it so often,* she thought wryly.

"Irsht said that we're making good time," she remarked, hoping to hide her unsettled feelings.

"Yes, we are," he agreed. "If we keep going at this pace, we should pull into the Stalli foothills in three days. Burkin Village is only a half day's ride from there."

"Only three and a half more days?" she asked, swiveling on her horse's back to stare at Crispin.

"Isn't that good?" he asked. "Don't you want to get out of the desert and into your new home?"

"I can't wait to see Wasso Lake, but I like the desert too," she answered honestly. "I was thinking of my parents. They still hurt over leaving the Root Forest people."

"Oh, they'll get over that once they make friends with other Stallis," Crispin said easily. "They've just forgotten what normal people are like."

Abruptly, Lacht twisted forward again and stared at the desert reaches. The excitement of the trip may have distracted her, but she remembered her last sight of the Root people standing at the edge of their forest. She remembered it quite vividly.

Some of them had waved, but most had stood very still, only their eyes showing the depth of their sadness. Those big gray eyes had resembled the shadowy root caves in their forest home; eye caves filled with shadows deep and mysterious and very sad at that time over the departure of the family they loved.

"We will never forget the Root Forest people," she said in a tone that matched Crispin's for evenness.

He doesn't understand, she thought quietly. Crispin had not had enough time with the strange people her family had lived with for twelve years. He didn't know them. How could he understand!

The young man next to her shifted on his horse, and she knew it was a new experience for him to have her stare straight ahead and correct him. He didn't seem to like it.

"I wonder if anyone's found that missing child yet," he mentioned, changing the subject.

She smiled, as eager for the change of subject as he was. "I certainly hope so! Do you think the Wassandra would let us know if they found her?"

"I like that word *us*," he told her, winking again.

"Well, do you?" she asked again, her face staying pink even though the sunset was now fading.

"I think so. Of course, we'd get news quicker if we had a Wet One who could go under the lake. The message box has its limitations."

"What's a Wet One?" she asked.

Crispin smiled broadly, as if relieved to see her wide-eyed and questioning again. "I can't really answer that question," he answered, his voice sinking deeper and his hand gesturing dramatically. "According to the stories, a few of our ancestors could breathe under the waters of Wasso Lake just like the Wassandra—and the water didn't get them wet!"

"How could a Stalli possibly breathe under water?" she asked. Then, before he could answer, she added, "You have got to tell Irsht and the others about this tonight!"

"I will," he agreed, pleased at the prospect, "though your mother must already know. Speaking of night, we should stop and make camp."

He jumped off his horse, picked up a warm handful of sand, and briskly rubbed it over the sweaty places on the horse's back and side. The horse grunted appreciation, then moved off into the rapidly darkening evening.

The other travelers caught up, and the general bustle of pitching tents and preparing supper prevented any further questions, but Lacht didn't forget. When they'd cleaned up and gathered around the campfire to relax, she waved her hands to get everyone's attention.

"Crispin told me something new today," she said, and her eyes shone in the flickering firelight.

Irsht would love this.

"People called the Wet Ones lived long ago and could breathe under Wasso Lake just like the Wassandra! Go on, Crispin, tell us more."

"I don't know anything more than that," he admitted

cheerfully. "Wet Ones walked under the lake without getting wet. Nobody knows much about them."

"That doesn't make sense! How could they go into water and not get wet? Besides, even if they could, Stallis wouldn't have called them 'Wet Ones.' They would've called them 'Dry Ones,'" commented practical Irsht, immediately as interested as her sister had predicted.

"They stepped in, stepped out, and their feet stayed as dry as the desert sand," Crispin insisted, his hand making a perfect semi-circle in the air. "I don't know why they were called Wet Ones, though. Dry Ones does seem a better name."

"Wet Ones," mused Frenne. "I'd forgotten about them. My grandmother used to say that they could walk into Wasso Lake as if strolling down an incline on dry land. The water didn't buoy them up as it did the other Stallis."

"Stallis!" exclaimed Irsht, lowering her cup so suddenly that hot mallowberry juice sloshed out of it. The person sitting next to her inched away, but she didn't notice. "You don't mean they were Stallis! Did they look different; strange, you know?"

"I've never seen one of them," answered her mother, dimples showing as she smiled at her youngest daughter's question.

"Probably pale and skinny," Crispin suggested, "with long fingers and webs between their toes."

The two girls shuddered while their father frowned. Lacht winced expectantly, but Winnel didn't say anything. He never did say much to Crispin, she'd noticed; nor did Crispin have much to say to him. She shrugged.

Different personality types, she told herself and refused to think about it.

That night, in the family tent, Irsht brought up the subject again.

"I can't wait to see this golden lake for myself," she said, unrolling her blanket. "I wish Wet Ones lived in our day and time, so they could tell us about the Wassandra."

"You never know when a Wet One will come along," Frenne informed her. "My grandmother said that Stalli children all hoped to be Wet Ones; until, of course, that first time they splashed in the lake and got their feet wet."

"Well, things must have changed since then," Irsht chattered on. "I can't imagine Crispin wanting to be a Wet One, can you? Besides, you could spot a Wet One in a minute, because he'd be pale and thin, and if you took his shoes off—"

"Irsht," Winnel scolded. "You don't believe that absurd description Crispin gave us, do you?"

"Not necessarily," she answered promptly without a trace of embarrassment. "However, no one has seen a Wet One in years. Who knows what they're like!"

"Keshua knows," her father stated in his don't-argue-with-me voice, "because he made them, just as he made the Paigens and the Muntas and the Root Forest people. Everyone doesn't have to look like a Stalli!"

Irsht stopped talking, though Lacht knew her younger sister wasn't convinced; and the family snuggled into their blankets. The desert air turned cold after dark, especially to people accustomed to the sheltered warmth of the Root Forest.

She pulled the thick blanket up around her face and yawned. Riding a horse all day was more tiring than any of them had expected. Normally, Lacht fell asleep right after her second yawn. Sometimes, her body didn't even change positions during the night.

Yawning again, she drifted off, but the normal sleep pattern ended there.

Three

The Second Dream

In the middle of the night, Lacht woke up; at least, she thought she did, but she wasn't in the tent anymore. She stood in the middle of vague, wavy things—then her vision cleared, and the wavy things took on the shape of long, dark red leaves.

Tarth's leaves were always blue except for a brief time in autumn, when they turned purple or pink. The unnatural color of these leaves bothered Lacht, even in her dream, and she cringed away from their touch. The red leaves grew unnaturally long too, because they started high above her and waved and curled all the way to her feet.

Without warning, something outside of the leaves started coming toward her, something that threw fear knives at her. She twisted in agony as the knives cut into her mind.

Suddenly, someone shrieked, "Help me! Please help me. I can't get out. Help—"

Lacht found herself sitting up in the tent, panting like a wounded animal. Her mother and Irsht threw off their blankets and put their arms around her. Her father lit a candle.

"What was it, child?" Winnel asked calmly.

"A dream, a bad dream," she gasped out.

She couldn't get enough air.

"It must have been a really bad dream. You should have heard yourself scream," Irsht said in a shaky voice unlike any Lacht had heard from her practical little sister.

Who could blame her! Practicality had its limits, after all, especially at night in the middle of desert wastes, with a pack of timidogs wailing not far away. The candle gave a little light, but not much, and the shadows it made wavered back and forth.

"There now, you've had bad dreams before," Frenne comforted her girls.

"Not here," Irsht whimpered, expressing the thought Lacht would have uttered if she'd been able to speak.

Winnel reached over and took his youngest daughter's hand. "We can sleep as safely here as we did in our Root Forest cave," he assured her. "Keshua loves us, sweetlings. He will take care of us wherever we are."

Neither girl objected to the childish nickname as they might have under different circumstances. Winnel's faith in Keshua was not only comforting, it was contagious.

Lacht's breathing began to slow down.

Irsht yawned. "Is there anything to eat?" she asked in her normal tone. "I'm starving!"

Everyone laughed, and Frenne reached for a supply pack. "When we left the Root Forest, our Paigen friends gave us a gift that I've been saving for a special time. I think this is that time."

The candle flame revealed a small flat bundle. Frenne unwrapped its protective covering, and a distinctive smell filled the tent, making every mouth in the tent water.

"Cinnamon stickies," Irsht cried out. "I want one!"

"Everyone all right in there?" asked a Munta from outside the tent, and Lacht blushed to think how loudly she must have screamed.

"We're fine," her father called out. "It was only a bad dream."

"Good," the Munta man answered and left to return to his own tent.

"Um, I thought you'd share our cinnamon stickies," Irsht said thickly, her mouth already full of the treat. "We don't have enough as it is."

Frenne laughed. "We have a whole box full."

"Not enough," insisted the indomitable girl. "I'm almost ready for another one."

Lacht ate a cinnamon stickie and lay back down, but she didn't sleep well the rest of the night. She couldn't forget this dream as easily as she'd dismissed the first one.

Winnel and Frenne dressed in the dark before the sun rose and went outside to start a fire. The girls waited until they could hear flames crackle, then pulled on their clothes underneath the blankets. Shivering, they wrapped blue shawls about their shoulders, knowing well that a half-hour's sunlight would heat the desert world so thoroughly, they'd pack the shawls away for the rest of the day.

"What did you dream about?" Irsht asked before they left the tent.

Lacht sat on the blanket she'd just rolled, glad her sister had waited until morning to ask. "All these long red leaves waved in the air, and something started coming at me. Then a voice said, 'Help me, help me.'" Her dream seemed stupid when she put it into words, and she hastened to add, "It was scarier than it sounds."

"Oh, it sounds pretty bad," Irsht assured her, "though I've had worse."

Lacht rolled her eyes. Irsht hadn't had a bad dream since she was three years old. She was too practical to have bad dreams.

Irsht ignored her older sister's skepticism. "All that talk about the Wassandra last night must have reminded you that they asked for help to find their missing girl. You're too imaginative, and the whole thing got into your dreams."

"I dreamed the same thing a week ago," Lacht confessed, "the night Crispin came to the cave for supper."

"You see," Irsht said, nodding with a satisfied air. "That's when he first told us about the missing girl. Don't worry; it'll pass.

Just try to be smart and sensible, like me!"

Lacht laughed and shook her head, but something in the explanation bothered her, though she didn't know what. Hurrying out of the tent, she welcomed the distractions involved in cooking breakfast and folding up the tent.

Not until she'd mounted her horse for another day of traveling did Lacht realize what was bothering her.

It was a girl. In my dream.

She shifted uneasily on the mare's back. Irsht had dismissed the whole thing easily enough, but then Irsht hadn't heard the girl shriek in terror.

I don't want to think about it.

Urging her mare forward, Lacht joined her sister and two of their Munta friends, but she didn't mention anything to Irsht then; nor did she mention anything later when they were alone.

She didn't have to—she already knew what Irsht would say.

"Yes, yes," Irsht would insist vigorously; "you dreamed about the missing girl. The whole thing resulted from an overactive imagination."

Undeniably, Lacht had an imagination, and a very active one!

She used it the rest of that day to picture the self-satisfaction that would envelop Irsht's face if, yet again, she proved herself right. Lacht could almost hear the triumph resounding in her sister's voice. The visual/audio image made her grin.

Who cares! It was only a dream.

They reached the foothills in three days, just as Crispin had predicted. Several herds of horses whinnied a greeting to their horses, who neighed enthusiastically back.

Lacht inhaled the fresh mountain air in long deep breaths, but both she and Irsht began shivering as Crispin led them up the first forested incline. Long before the day's warmth left the desert below them, they had unpacked their shawls.

That night, for the first time, the travelers pitched their tents under Stalli trees. Lacht walked away from the fire and stared upwards until she got a crick in her neck.

"Listen," she told her mother when she joined her.

"What is it?" asked the older woman after listening carefully. "What do you hear?"

"The leaves are so small. They whisper to each other," Lacht remarked, mesmerized by the rustling.

"I know. That's a sound I always loved," Frenne agreed. "I've missed it."

They stood and listened together for several minutes.

"What are you two doing?' asked Irsht, coming up behind them.

"Uh, uh, nothing," stuttered Frenne vaguely.

Lacht nodded and kept her mouth shut. The idea of telling Irsht, practical Irsht that they'd been listening to leaves whisper— *unthinkable!*

"Dad says we should go to bed even though it's early. He says tomorrow will be a big day," Irsht said, watching her older sister and mother suspiciously.

"What were you doing?" she asked again as they walked toward the tent.

"I'll never tell," Lacht stated immediately and emphatically as she pulled her shawl closer around her. "A hundred Root Forest slugs couldn't make me tell. You'd laugh."

"Oh, something stupid," Irsht responded, her face relaxing as she shrugged.

Obviously, she didn't need to know about something stupid.

Lacht never asked how well other people slept that night, but she lay awake for hours. The next day, they'd reach Burkin Village, their new home. She planned to wake up before anyone else that final morning, but her mother beat her to it.

Frenne rushed outside the tent and banged two pots together before the night sky showed any hint of morning light. "Get up," she shouted. "Get up so we can leave."

Winnel chuckled in the dark tent. He pushed back his blanket and deftly rolled it. "Your mother's excited," he pointed out, a little unnecessarily. "You might as well wake up."

"As if anyone could sleep through that noise," grumbled Irsht. "I thought it was a thunderstorm at first. Crispin says Stalli Mountain thunderstorms are the loudest storms on Tarth."

Lacht had already hopped up, rolled her blanket, and tied it to Winnel's. As soon as the two girls dressed and stumbled outside the tent, Irsht stared pointedly up at the whirling nightlights.

"If the Muntas hadn't left us yesterday, would you still have banged those pots together?" she asked her mother grumpily.

"Why not?" answered her mother hurriedly. "I'm sure they would've appreciated an early start to their day. Do you folks want something to eat, or shall we just pack up and leave right away?"

After loud assurances that her family did, indeed, want something to eat, Frenne settled down to the business of preparing breakfast. She wasn't over her excitement, though.

Lacht grimaced as she sipped a cup of hot water. She felt certain her mother had meant to give her tea, but somehow the tea leaves had never reached the cup, and Frenne had packed the breakfast supplies away five minutes ago.

At least it's hot, she thought resignedly.

Frenne ate a few bites, then hovered over her family until they'd finished. She had the breakfast things cleaned and packed before the rest of them had taken down the tents.

Crispin beamed as if personally complimented by her excitement. "Your mother's great," he told Lacht when they had finally packed and mounted their horses.

"Most of the time," she cautiously agreed.

"All of the time!" he corrected her with a smile. "I can't blame her for wanting to get to Burkin Village. It's the most—"

"Beautiful village in Stalli," Irsht finished for him, coming up behind them on her horse. "Yeah, yeah, we've heard."

"Wait till you see it for yourself," he told her, flourishing his hand in the air twice.

♫ ♫ ♫

They reached the first cottages a little before noon. Irsht and Lacht stared, and Lacht clutched the mane of her horse with both hands. The cottages were either blue with gray shutters or gray with blue shutters. Some of them had signs on their front doors.

Shops!

They hadn't had shops in the Root Forest. They hadn't had cottages in the Root Forest. Root people lived in hidden root caves spread far apart under the sheltering trees.

I could get down now.

Irsht had dismounted long before Lacht finished her wide-eyed survey of the new place. Everyone had dismounted, she noticed, with a flushed face.

Her mare flicked an ear back toward her but stood without moving, letting Lacht adjust to the new surroundings.

"Thanks," she murmured in acknowledgment but didn't release her fistfuls of mane.

"Lacht," Winnel finally called.

The eighteen-year-old glanced in her father's direction and made herself slide to the ground. At least she wasn't blushing anymore. In fact, her face didn't feel as if it had any color left in it at all. She hugged her horse's neck one last time, then had to step back quickly.

Free at last, the mare danced and snorted with excitement as she waited for these humans to unload her friends. The unloading didn't take long. In minutes, all the Stalli Mountain horses raced at a gallop into their forest home.

The horses set the pace for the day, because, after they left, everything raced at a gallop, especially Frenne.

"We have a choice between two empty cottages," Frenne called to her family, the words galloping out of her mouth. "Let's go see them."

No sooner did Irsht and Lacht reach the first cottage, a gray two-story on the outskirts of the village, than Frenne, who had managed to get there before them, dashed out the door and said, "All right, let's go to the other cottage. I'm sure we'll take it anyway! We don't need something this big, though the other one's well needs cleaning, I hear."

Sighing, the girls trudged through the unfamiliar roads to the second cottage, a one-story blue one with gray shutters. Frenne, of course, had gotten there first and charged out the front door just as they stepped onto the porch.

"Yes, we should take this one, despite the dirty well. We'll drink mallowberry juice and boil water until someone can clean it for us. Don't you think so, Lacht?"

She gave her mother a fierce look. "I haven't been inside yet."

"Oh, yes. Well, you go on in while I start unloading our things," Frenne chattered. "The carts should get here soon. I'll walk back and help push!"

Lacht had never seen her mother this excited. She didn't think she liked the new Frenne, but she needn't have worried. By the time they'd unloaded everything, her mother had relaxed.

They ate a late afternoon supper since they'd skipped lunch, then sat on the porch.

When a few neighbors stopped by to visit, Lacht slipped down the porch steps.

"I think I'll take a walk," she murmured and left with a headache, yearning for the comfortable familiarity of old friends.

Crispin almost counted as an old friend now, but he'd left as soon as they reached Burkin Village and hadn't returned all that busy afternoon. Irsht had met two girls her own age and gone off with them after supper, the three girls laughing and chattering together. Lacht's parents had made new friends already, as well.

I'll make friends too, she thought with a decided nod, but that didn't make her headache go away.

She wandered through the village, deliberately keeping to the side roads, because fewer people used them. When one of the roads ended in trees, Lacht didn't hesitate. She couldn't wait to get away from all these cottages and people.

Plunging between two trees, she felt better right away; at least, her headache ebbed within the familiar privacy of a forest. At the same time though, her throat tightened. The damp leaves smelled like the Root Forest.

She walked fast and tried to empty her mind.

Suddenly, without any warning from the trees, which grew as close together as ever, she found herself teetering on the edge of a steep downward slope. Clutching at a low hanging branch, the homesick girl stopped herself from falling headlong, but she had to sit down hard on the slope's top edge.

Lacht sat. She didn't try to get up. She sat very still on the top of the slope and stared, her mouth dropping open.

At the bottom of the bank, shimmering in the early evening light, swirled the golden mists of Wasso Lake. She couldn't see the water. The mists completely covered both the surface of the lake and the lower third of the bank. Lacht sat and stared at the misty curls of gold until the light faded; then with a sigh, she got up.

"I have to go now," she told the lake, "but I'll come back tomorrow."

The wood gave her no trouble on the way back. Lacht had grown up in a forest, after all, and was woods-wise. She was not, however, roads-wise. Three times she made a wrong turn on the village roads and had to retrace her steps; but finally, when Stalli nightlights danced in all their fullness above her, she came in sight of her new home.

A running, panting Irsht greeted her. "Guess what I saw?"

Without waiting for a reply, Irsht answered her own question. "I saw Wasso Lake, and it's covered with these weird mists that move as if there's a wind, when there isn't any wind. I can't believe people live under that water—if they're what you'd call 'people'! I'm glad we got this cottage and not one of the closer ones. You can see the lake from their porches."

"What?" Lacht responded immediately, wishing they could move again. "I went to the lake too, but I didn't see any nearby cottages. Where did you go?"

"Oh, down some road over there," her sister said, waving vaguely in the air.

"Girls," their mother called. "I found your sheets."

"Coming," Irsht called back and grabbed Lacht's arm as they walked to their door. "Didn't you think the mists were weird?"

"No, I thought they were beautiful!"

Irsht stared at her for a minute, then changed the subject. "Crispin came by."

Lacht lost the faraway look. "What?" she asked again, more alert. "When did he come? Where is he now?"

"I guess he's home, wherever that is," Irsht replied matter-of-factly. "I think he might have helped us unpack."

"He's got family too, you know," Lacht said, defending her friend. "Maybe he wanted to see them."

Crispin's mother and father had died several years ago, leaving him with an older married sister and a younger brother. He'd talked about them on the trip across the desert. Meddy, the sister, bossed the two boys around, he'd announced.

"That's all right, Crispin," Irsht had commiserated. "All older sisters are bossy."

Lacht had laughed loudly. Even Winnel and Frenne had chuckled. Irsht was much more bossy than Lacht, and everyone knew it.

Crispin had winked at Lacht and continued talking. His

younger brother had hurt one of his legs as a child and limped badly ever since. When they got older, he and Crispin had started a wood and metal business.

"Ploddin can design an iron gate with such lifelike flowers that people bend to smell them as they walk past. He's the best metal worker on Tarth! He doesn't get along with people, though. I do most of the selling."

Crispin is good with people, Lacht thought warmly as she and Irsht climbed the porch steps of their new home. *Of course, he wanted to greet his family and friends.*

The front door opened off the porch into a big kitchen that dominated the whole house. Behind the kitchen, two small bedrooms snuggled together across a short hall from a sitting room. Cobwebs hung everywhere, and Lacht felt as if she were wading through several layers of dust, but the place had a cozy feel. She liked it.

In their new bedroom, the sisters made up their beds side by side.

"Is this room really any bigger than our cave room?" Irsht asked critically when they'd finished and stepped back to see the results of their labors.

Two steps and their backs brushed a wall.

"Well, it has a window," Lacht pointed out. "The cave didn't have any windows. I think an outside view makes a small room seem bigger."

"That's true." Irsht yawned. "I'm going to bed."

Lacht didn't feel tired, but she got ready for bed anyway. She lay curled under her blankets, staring out the window at the Tarth nightlights that spun and twisted inside their circles, moving ceaselessly. They reminded her of the golden mists swirling up the bank of Wasso Lake.

No, I didn't think the mists were weird.

Four

The Wet One

The next morning, everyone slept late except Frenne, who got up early again so she could organize her kitchen.

Irsht lay in bed grumbling at the noise two pans made as they banged against each other—accidentally, this time. But both girls hopped up when the delicious smell of toasting sweetbread, a gift from a generous neighbor, spread throughout the house.

Stalli sweetbread, filled with nuts, topped with dried fruits, and dripping with butter and honey was a treat reserved for special occasions. Lacht and Irsht had always requested it on their birthdays.

Actually, they'd requested it many more times than that, but Frenne had laughed at them and told them to wait until someone proposed. The asking sweetbread and accepting sweetbread were an old Stalli tradition.

Lacht sniffed appreciatively as she threw on her clothes and hurried down the short hall. Sweetbread smelled good even cold, but toasted sweetbread filled the senses with an aroma that left little room for anything else. Not until she'd entered the kitchen did she smell the spicy fragrance of tea.

Her mother smiled from the stove as she scooped scrambled eggs onto a platter. Then Irsht and Winnel rushed into the kitchen behind Lacht, sniffing hungrily.

Frenne pointed toward a jar of preserved blueberries she'd

placed on the counter. "I'm making a special breakfast to celebrate the first morning in our new home," she announced.

Winnel smiled at his wife. "You're a wonderful woman!"

"Yes, yes, yes, you certainly are," agreed Irsht, heading purposefully for the counter. "Just wonderful! Now let me put those blueberries on the table for you."

"Don't let her touch them, Mom," shouted Lacht. "You know Irsht!"

The whole family scrambled for the jar, but Winnel was the one who emerged victorious.

"I, myself, will escort this jar of blueberries to the table, and, thereafter, stand personal guard over it," he informed his disappointed younger daughter.

"I've never seen such a family," Irsht complained. "I offer to help, and everyone goes wild. All right, I'll get the sweetbread."

When they pulled up the chairs that went with the old kitchen table, several bottom rungs popped right out of their holes. Sticking the short sticks of wood back in was easy enough, but the girls tentatively lowered themselves onto the chair seats and didn't dare lean back.

The table itself teetered dangerously whenever anyone rested an arm on it.

Lacht hoped silently that the table and chairs would last through breakfast, and somehow they did, but the kitchen furniture's time of usefulness had basically ended.

"I'll talk to someone this morning about making a new table and chairs," Winnel promised.

"You should ask Crispin and his brother, Ploddin," suggested Lacht. "They work with wood. I'll go with you!"

Irsht smirked meaningfully at her sister's eagerness but only asked, "Why would they call a lame boy *Ploddin*? All he could do was plod along, and they had to name him for it?"

"His parents named him before the accident," Winnel reminded her. "Ploddin is a common enough name. We should have both boys over for supper soon."

34

"Give me a week," begged Frenne. "I've all kinds of cleaning to do."

Irsht nodded immediately. She liked to clean. Lacht had always thought it one of her sister's most outstanding virtues.

Not long after breakfast, Lacht, who did not like to clean, left the cottage with her father. As they walked down the porch steps, they could hear Frenne and Irsht making happy comments to each other about the dirt. Lacht and Winnel smiled at each other in complete understanding.

How nice that our loved ones enjoy cleaning! How nice that we can leave while our loved ones enjoy cleaning!

They took a full hour to reach Crispin and Ploddin's shop, because Winnel couldn't simply stop and ask directions. He had to get to know everyone he met. Lacht forced back a sigh more than once; but, at last, they walked into the front yard of a gray cottage with a blue sign on its door that read, *Wood and Metal.*

They didn't need to knock. A young man sat at an outdoors forge, examining something that might be a garden hoe once he had finished it.

"Ploddin?" asked Winnel.

The man glanced up and puckered his lips. Lacht thought immediately of Mudde, but this man was too young to look as if he'd bit into a sourplum.

"Yes," he answered shortly.

"My name is Winnel, and this is my daughter, Lacht. We're new to Burkin Village and find ourselves in need of a table and chairs. Would you make them for us?"

Ploddin wrinkled his forehead and shook his head, but before he could answer, the door banged open.

"Of course we will!" boomed a familiar voice as Crispin bounded down the porch steps. "Hello, Winnel. Lacht, how do you like Burkin Village?"

"Just fine," she responded weakly, feeling as if she needed to sit somewhere.

Crispin often had this effect on her. Energy burst out of him to such an extent that it drained her own energy level, but she didn't mind. She infinitely preferred his broad smile to his brother's mopey countenance.

"We have a full quota of back orders," warned Ploddin sharply, the edges of his mouth shooting downward. "It will take us a month or two to get to these people."

Lacht bristled at the words, "these people," but Winnel only nodded.

"Take your time," he said. "We'll wait our turn. I can make our table and chairs last until you get to us."

Putting together the full combination of puckered lips, wrinkled forehead, and downward curving mouth, Ploddin stared at Winnel. Lacht tensed with dislike. If he dared talk rudely to her father—

Fortunately, Winnel had his usual way with a grouchy person. She didn't know how her father did it, but she'd seen it happen too many times to doubt it. Ploddin didn't smile, but his lips lost their pucker and the lines on his forehead smoothed out.

"In that case, we'll take your order," he agreed.

"Of course, we will," shouted Crispin. "Lacht, let me show you around the village!"

"I'd like that," she stammered, "but aren't you busy? I mean, you have all those back orders."

"Oh, Ploddin will keep working," he assured her.

Much as she liked Crispin, Lacht couldn't help but notice the unfairness of this arrangement. She hesitated, glancing over at Ploddin. He glanced back at her.

"Go ahead," he said briefly.

"Thanks," she responded softly.

"Umpht," grunted Ploddin as he lifted the end of the hoe and started fitting it into a wooden handle.

The brief exchange ended, but Lacht knew, as she waved good-bye to her father and left, that she'd lost her irritation towards the grumpy young man. She knew, in fact, that when she saw Ploddin next, she'd feel quite relaxed around him, as if she'd known him much longer than ten minutes.

Crispin gave Lacht a tour of the small village that left her breathless. They visited in the homes of everyone he knew well, and since Crispin knew most people well, the morning became early afternoon before she knew it.

He cajoled several young people into joining them for a picnic lunch at the lake, then led the way to the home of his sister, Meddy, whose cottage sat directly across the road from Wasso Lake.

Surrounded by the group of young people, Lacht caught only a glimpse of gold before she climbed Meddy's porch steps, but that glimpse made her wish again that her family could move. She wanted to trade cottages with someone, build a new one, anything to get within sight of the beautiful water.

The group had brought bread, meat, cheese, lettuce, and pickles; and they proceeded to take over Meddy's kitchen. While they made their sandwiches, Crispin entertained them with little-known facts about the Wassandra. Lacht suspected that most of his facts came into existence right before he shared them.

She wasn't the only one with an overdose of imagination!

"Finish your sandwiches, my friends," the handsome Stalli man told them. "We have a job to do. We must keep guard over our village as we watch for Wassandra." Crispin spoke his last words in a low, quavering that brought appreciative shudders to a few.

"I am quite certain you won't see any," Meddy remarked. She had not appreciatively shuddered at her brother's words, and now her eyebrows rose to form two sarcastic triangles. "Doubtlessly, Wassandra work during the day."

Lacht looked askance at her. Meddy had enough family resemblance to Crispin and Ploddin to make her an attractive, middle-aged woman, with glossy black hair and straight white teeth, but she'd scowled at Crispin ever since their small group had arrived. Obviously, Lacht wasn't the only one to notice that he'd left Ploddin with all the work to do.

Crispin smiled ingratiatingly. "We're working," he insisted. "We're searching for that missing Wassandra girl."

"Oh, you mean the girl is still lost?" Lacht asked, breaking into the conversation and wondering why Irsht hadn't found this out yesterday.

Is Irsht sick? She always finds things out.

"We don't know," Meddy answered her. "The Wassandra haven't brought us another message."

The woman's eyebrows relaxed, Lacht noticed, when she stopped talking to Crispin.

Lacht nodded, slapping a piece of bread on top of the sandwich she'd made and putting it in the basket. She understood Irsht's silence now. Her sister had doubtlessly found the lake's swirling mists more interesting than a complete lack of news.

"That Wassandra girl could have turned up a long time ago," a Burkin Village boy said in disgust. "They wouldn't have to tell us, you know."

"She is still missing," Crispin said in high good humor. "In some mysterious pocket of the lake, she waits for us to find her. Let's go!"

The group had finished making their sandwiches. They left in a rush, but Lacht lingered.

She hadn't minded leaving her mother and sister at home with all the cleaning. Irsht and Frenne loved cleaning. Barging into someone else's cottage, making a mess, and then leaving, however, was another matter.

Quickly, she got a dishrag and started to wipe crumbs off the table.

"Lacht, are you coming?" came a shout from outside the cottage.

Only Crispin could make a noise that loud!

"In a minute," she called back and kept on brushing crumbs into her hand.

She finished wiping the table, threw away the crumbs, and straightened up to find Meddy staring at her with evident appreciation.

"Thank you," Meddy said with more warmth than Lacht had heard the Stalli woman use yet.

Another shout came from outside. "You don't want us to find the missing girl without you, do you?"

The older woman glanced toward the door. "Precious amount of time that bunch will spend looking for anything but a good time," she muttered.

Lacht hesitated. The group had filled the kitchen sink with dirty knives and plates.

"Go on," Meddy told her briskly. "Come back later when we can visit."

Lacht smiled broadly. She'd made a friend. "I will," she promised and ran down the porch steps.

She'd meant to catch up quickly with the group waiting twenty feet away—but her feet stopped short before they left the road, and her lips parted with a gasp.

A meadow lay between the cottages and the lake, a meadow that swooped gracefully downwards as if it were a bird in flight.

Lacht had never seen a shapely land curve. The Root Forest lay perfectly flat; and though the desert rose and fell, its sandy swells curved gently, almost imperceptibly.

She'd ridden over the Stalli foothills, of course, but trees had covered those hills, trees with small blue leaves that whispered to each other. Preoccupied with the whispering leaves, Lacht hadn't noticed the shape of the hills. She'd never paid attention to the shape of any land.

She did now. Thick blue grass accentuated the curving meadow, growing much shorter than the tall blades that grew wild in the woods.

The grass spread out before her like a luxurious rug.

Automatically, she stepped forward, until the spongy softness was beneath her feet. It felt good even through shoes. The blue rug hugged the meadow's slope all the way down to a wide expanse of golden water.

Lacht wanted to stand very still and stare, but her new friends shouted her on, so she hurried to catch up with them, and the group ran down the meadow.

As they drew closer, Lacht could see a constant swirling movement that rippled across the lake. The mists must retreat into the water in the middle of the day. She couldn't see beneath the surface, though. Whatever went on in Wasso Lake stayed hidden from view.

"Let's eat!" bellowed Crispin.

"How can we expect to spot Wassandra when you keep making all that noise?" one of his friends teased him.

They sat towards the bottom of the meadow and ate their sandwiches. Lacht ate quietly, gazing about her and listening to more stories about the lake and its strange inhabitants.

"Wassandra ride on animals they have lured into the lake. With one look from their hypnotic eyes, they make the animals forget purple skies and blue trees," Crispin said in his best creepy voice.

"The imprisoned beasts live underwater the rest of their lives until their shapes become warped and strange. Stay away from the golden water when the mists are high," he finished with his patented hand flourish.

"The mists aren't high now!" proclaimed one of the girls, jumping to her feet. "I want to wade. Who's with me?"

The rest of the group rose to the challenge and flung off their shoes and socks. Lacht took hers off too, wiggling her toes in excitement.

With daring whoops, everyone rushed to the edge of Wasso Lake, but Lacht held back, not wanting to join the boisterous group this time. She wanted to wade slowly, taking delight in the beautiful water, not kicking it up into a hundred, sparkling drops of gold as Crispin was doing.

With deliberate focus, she put one foot into the shallow water, then the other. The surface wasn't completely opaque, after all. She could see two or three inches below the surface, which meant she could see the tops of her feet, not the bottoms; however, that didn't explain why she didn't feel a change of temperature against her skin.

Everyone else was complaining loudly about the cold water. Several of them had started hopping up and down to help their feet adjust.

Lacht couldn't feel a thing. Well, she could feel the sandy lake bottom, but nothing above that. All of a sudden, she jumped out of the water and stared with unnaturally wide eyes at her feet.

Turning, she dashed up the meadow to where they'd left their things.

"Where are you going?" called Crispin.

"Home," she answered without turning.

"Don't leave," he begged. "We might go swimming. It's not dangerous if we stay together. Our clothes get wet, but the sun dries them in no time."

"I have to go home," she said and picked up her shoes and socks with trembling hands.

Not until she'd run up the sloping meadow and reached the village road did Lacht stop to put her shoes on. She didn't need to wipe her feet.

They were perfectly dry, as dry as the desert sands; and both feet had been perfectly dry when she first stepped out of the water of Wasso Lake.

Five

The Third Dream

"D on't you want to come with me?" asked Irsht
plaintively.

Five days ago, they'd arrived in Burkin Village. After
the first day, Lacht had stayed close by their cottage, refusing all
invitations to go anywhere.

"No," she responded now, smiling slightly, but the smile
didn't warm her eyes. "I have more work to do on the yard."

"What do you mean, more work?" argued Irsht. "It would
take a year to get this yard in shape."

"Good," Lacht told her. "Then I'll take a year."

Irsht cocked her head. "You fought with Crispin, didn't you?"

"No," her sister said again, turning away and picking up her
shovel.

"But you won't go anywhere, even with him. I thought you
liked him."

"Everyone likes Crispin," answered Lacht, but the old
excitement had left her voice.

Irsht couldn't figure this one out. She watched as Lacht put a
foot on top of the shovel's blade and tried to push it into the
ground, bending almost double with the effort. One side of Irsht's
mouth tightened; then suddenly, she leaned over and kissed her
sister's cheek.

Lacht straightened up quickly. A long look passed between
them. Then the older girl smiled, and this time her eyes warmed.

Irsht nodded. It would do for now. "Well, I'll walk over to the store. Do you want some flower bulbs?"

"What? Oh yeah, sure," Lacht replied with a shrug, as if she didn't really care.

Irsht left, shaking her head.

An hour later, Lacht straightened her back, stared down at her left hand, and groaned. She'd developed another blister.

Her father came out the kitchen door in time to hear her groan. His forehead tightened, and she knew his concern wasn't due to her blister, at least not solely. The foreheads of everyone in her family tightened when they saw her these days.

"I'm going to visit Ploddin at the shop," he told her. "Want to come?"

She sighed. They were all making an effort to get her away from the cottage. It was a conspiracy, a definite conspiracy.

Shrugging slightly, she nodded. "All right. I'm not doing any good here."

"You've made progress," her father said mildly, "but you need a mattock to loosen the soil, not a shovel. I'll find you one."

"It doesn't matter," she muttered, but she walked down the road feeling a little better.

Winnel always made her feel better. Maybe that was why she could go somewhere with him. He loved her, but he wouldn't try to ferret out her problem. She could relax around him.

When they reached the shop, Ploddin was sitting at the outdoors forge again; but this time he held a complicated arrangement of iron bars in his hands. Lacht sat next to her father on an old, wooden crate and watched while the young man hammered.

The bars seemed a tangled mess to Lacht, and she kept staring at them even after Ploddin lifted his head and acknowledged their visit with a nod.

"It's a gate, isn't it?" she guessed before her father could greet the young man.

Ploddin snorted. "A gate! Is this something you'd want to walk through?" he asked with a glimmer of humor.

"A porch railing?" asked Lacht.

The amused glimmer grew as the young blacksmith shook his head.

"A new kind of garden hoe?" she guessed randomly.

"Now you're getting closer," he informed her. "I'm making a plow that will turn soil and break up dirt clods at the same time."

"I thought it was a piece of iron artwork," Winnel admitted ruefully. "From this angle, it looks like a woman hanging up wash on a windy day."

Ploddin couldn't stop a low chuckle from breaking its way out of him. His face lightened briefly.

Lacht grinned and poked her father in the ribs. "I was closer than you," she pointed out.

When she glanced back toward Ploddin, the amused expression had vanished, but his face stayed lighter than normal.

"Do you have a question, or are you visiting?" he asked.

"Visiting," Winnel answered comfortably from the crate. "Does it bother you when people watch you work?"

"No one's ever wanted to," Ploddin remarked, bending his head to the plow again.

He studied it intently, then put one section into the fire. When it glowed red, he drew it out and skillfully hammered the piece of metal into an *S* shape.

Lacht's attention wandered to the little yard.

A child would have loved playing there. Metal pieces of all sizes and shapes bulged out of one corner, while wood lay loosely piled in another. What resembled a contrivance for pulling things sat near the road. Someone must have brought it in for repairs.

The outdoors forge sizzled in a way that reminded her of melvefish fillets frying in a pan of hot oil. She could feel the fire's

heat from where they sat, but she didn't mind—on the contrary!
Lacht liked heat. She'd grown up in the Root Forest, after all; and
the high altitude of her new home often gave her the shivers.

The forge sent another gusty wave of heat across the yard, and
she yawned as she turned her gaze toward the small cottage. The
Wood and Metal sign hung right in the middle of the door, flanked
on either side by the usual Stalli porch, with three steps leading to
the yard. Under the bottom step stared two eyes.

Lacht blinked.

The eyes were still there, staring at her. She stared intently
back and could just barely see the outline of a small dog lying
motionless in the shadows.

"Well," Winnel said, standing up and stretching.

Both Lacht and the dog jumped.

"I think I'll visit Pudca. She's sick again, I hear."

Ploddin glanced up but made no comment. Lacht didn't even
know who Pudca was. Leave it to her father to find someone who
needed comforting.

"Coming, Lacht?" asked Winnel.

She shook her head.

"I'll see you at home, then," he said and walked off.

Lacht knew her father planned to start a new rope later that
afternoon. Burkin Village hadn't had a rope maker for three years.
Already, he had a waiting list as long as Ploddin's, but Winnel
wouldn't let that stop him from visiting sick people—or grouches.

She looked back under the porch. The two eyes had risen
above the bottom step now. The little dog must have sat up.

"Your father's all right," Ploddin said.

Lacht nodded agreement, and he continued working; though
she didn't know how anyone could work so energetically that
close to the hot forge. She felt like taking a nap, and she wasn't
nearly as close to the fire.

"What's your dog's name?" she finally asked.

"What? Oh, that's Brownie," Ploddin said, jerking his head
toward the porch steps. "He's not my dog, but he likes to sleep

under the porch, and I feed him."

She cocked her head.

"He sleeps here and you feed him, but he's not your dog?"

"That's right," Ploddin maintained casually before he saw her face. "Brownie doesn't like people," he added quickly.

"Well, that's one thing the two of you have in common," his visitor commented. "Have you tried to help him get over his social fears?"

"No," he answered, shaking his head in obvious confusion.

Obviously, no one had ever had this conversation with him.

High time, thought Lacht.

"And who named a perfectly respectable creature of Keshua's, 'Brownie'?" she asked next, staring at Ploddin.

"Well, he is brown."

The words fell feebly out of Ploddin's mouth, and Lacht raised her nose and sniffed. She moved across the yard and sat on the bottom step.

"I will rename him after I have made friends," she announced.

Ploddin stared at Lacht, then down at his plow.

He found the plow easier to understand, so he kept his eyes on it until he remembered what he had wanted to do next. That step led to another one, and he became engrossed in his work.

A half-hour passed before he straightened up again. Lacht was sitting on the ground now with her back against the side of the steps. He could see a little brown head in the shadows.

"He's right behind you," he murmured.

"I know," she whispered. "He came that close ten minutes ago, but he's scared to come any closer. I'm going to sing to him."

She glared at Ploddin, as if daring him to object. When he didn't say anything, she closed her eyes and started a children's song about rain making spring flowers grow. He listened to her sing it through three times before he remembered his plow.

Eying the hammer in his hand, the young blacksmith shook his head and decided to switch to woodcarving. He grabbed the edge of his bench to help him up, rose to his feet, and limped as quietly as he could across the yard. When he reached the steps, the singing stopped and Lacht looked up at him.

"Woodwork's less noisy," he explained.

She nodded and started singing again. He pulled himself up the steps and limped into the cottage to get his wood and the tools he needed. Then he came outside onto the porch again.

"Stay up there," came the calm order.

Ploddin paused. Whose cottage was this anyway? Unexpectedly, a grin lifted the edges of his mouth—the first real grin his face had experienced in years.

He sat in a porch chair and started carving a bedpost. Every so often he craned his neck to check below him, but Lacht had moved nearer to the porch now, and he couldn't see her any longer.

When she started talking to the dog, he knew her wooing had succeeded.

"Well, well, well," the Stalli girl crooned. "Is this a nose I see? Come out here. That's right, come out further, and let me look at you. My, aren't you a skinny little thing. Doesn't that mean man feed you enough?"

Ploddin snorted and heard her laugh in response.

"There, I knew he was eavesdropping. We'll make him feed you better, won't we, Brownie? Then we'll change your name. The idea of naming such a handsome, smart dog *Brownie!* It's outrageous, isn't it? Come on now, one more step. That's right."

On and on she murmured, and he pictured in his mind the small, brown body taking slow, cringing steps, its heart beating wildly. It wanted to approach the gentle, soft-spoken person but felt afraid, so afraid. Step by step, Ploddin listened to Lacht urge the dog on until, finally, she could stroke his head.

"I thought you'd feel soft," she murmured, and he knew from

her tone that she'd forgotten all about the eavesdropper.

"Would you like me to scratch behind your ears? Does that feel good? How about here? That's the best place, isn't it—on the tummy...yes, right on the little tummy."

The sound of people talking and laughing loudly in the distance interrupted them. Brownie disappeared into the shadows of the porch, and Lacht rose in one quick movement to her feet.

"I'm leaving," she told Ploddin. She hesitated, then asked, "May I come again tomorrow? Brownie needs more time."

He stared at her from the porch. "Am I a mean man?" he asked fiercely.

She started to smile. "No," she admitted.

"Do I feed Brownie enough?"

"Probably," she said, still smiling, "but he is thin."

"That," Ploddin announced, "is his own fault. He starts at every noise and runs off before he can finish eating."

Someone laughed loudly a block away, and Lacht's smile faded. She left, but before she reached the first corner, she turned around and waved.

Ploddin waved back, then realized he was sitting in his porch chair with the bedpost in one hand, the carving knife in the other, and a smile on his face. Immediately, he got rid of the smile and stood to put the other things away too. He could go back to his plow now.

Crispin and his friends came into view. Ploddin glanced towards them and spotted a small, brown body whip around the corner after Lacht. *He doesn't need as much time as you think,* he corrected the Stalli girl and grinned again.

Lacht felt almost like her old self at supper that night. She chatted to her family about the progress she'd made with Brownie.

"What could make a dog that shy?" wondered Irsht.

"Who knows?" answered her mother. "Someone might have mistreated him, or maybe he grew up wild. It's hard to make a wild animal realize it can trust you."

"Brownie trusts me," bragged Lacht, then qualified her statement. "At least, he's beginning to. I'll go over there every day until he does, but I can't change his name after all. I thought of Shadow, because he lives under the shadow of the porch, but I can't make the switch. He's Brownie to me now."

The conversation ebbed. Then Irsht straightened in her chair and made an announcement.

"I'm teaching school this fall."

"What?" gasped Frenne and Lacht.

Lacht wanted to laugh out loud. Irsht couldn't teach school. Irsht was her little sister.

"They need someone, and I think I can do it," Irsht said, her face glowing. "What do you think?" she asked Winnel.

"I think you'd make a fine teacher. You get along well with children, and you've always loved learning!" Winnel told his younger daughter. "A teacher should love to learn!"

"I think you'd make a good teacher too," Frenne quickly agreed. "What ages will you have?"

"The youngest ones," Irsht explained, "to give Masha more time with the others. She's going to help me with lesson plans, and I need to visit all my students before school starts. Summer's officially over in three weeks, you know. I've a lot to do before then," and practical Irsht shook her head over the situation, but her whole body glowed this time.

"Oh Irsht, that's great!" Lacht said.

She'd lost the desire to laugh. Her little sister had a grownup's job. It made Lacht feel insecure. *Everything makes me feel insecure,* she admitted with a grimace—*now.*

The rest of that night belonged to Irsht, though, and Lacht forgot herself in the general talk about art supplies and books. When she went to bed later than usual, she fell asleep quickly.

The third dream didn't frighten her as much as the first two; consequently, it lasted longer.

She stood in a small, enclosed place. Long leaves waved on all sides, but they didn't touch her this time, because she stood in the middle of a cave they had formed.

Lacht stared at the leaves closely. They'd begun to change color. The unusual dark red showed streaks of purple running up and down the length of the leaves. *They're too early,* she thought in her dream. *Fall shouldn't start for three more weeks.*

When she noticed the vague shape crouched on the ground beside her, she gave a tremendous start. That is, her mind gave a start. Her body, as often happens in dreams, did not move the way she wanted it to. It stood very still and stared wide-eyed at the small, balled-up shape.

No shrieking this time, she thought. *That's why I can't wake up.*

Her mind gave another start. The shape had begun talking in such a low tone that she could only hear a few words at first, but it grew louder toward the end. "Sorry...don't...turning purple...terrible, horrible...won't let me...Keshua, help...need you to...scared, I'm scared. Please, please, Keshua. Please, help me."

The shape squeezed itself into a tighter ball and started crying....

Lacht felt herself waking up, though she didn't feel frightened this time, only sad. Then she was awake, lying in her own bed, with Irsht's slow breathing next to her in the room. She knew that if she opened her eyes, she'd see nightlights swirling outside her window, but Lacht didn't open them. She'd cry if she opened them.

Poor person.

No, that wasn't right. She knew better than that.

Poor girl. Poor unhappy Wassandra girl. Keshua, please help her.

Six

An Old Grump

Lacht climbed up one more rung. The ladder wobbled under her, but she needed the extra height. Wetting her rag in the bucket of water balanced on top of the ladder, she scrubbed the upper half of her bedroom window.

Oh, root fungus! There's another bad spot.

The rag splashed back into the water, and she picked up the knife lying next to the bucket. Slanting the blade, she scraped off the layer of grunge that had accumulated over who knew how many years. Then, balancing carefully, she put the knife down, squeezed out her wet rag, and wiped the corner clean. She'd almost finished. Once she dried the glass so that the wet places wouldn't leave streak marks—

"Umph, no, come back here," she scolded loudly, making an unsuccessful grab at the towel hung on the other side of the ladder.

The towel, as if glad to escape, floated airily in the breezes to the far side of the yard and landed in a clump of weeds. Lacht groaned and clutched the top rung. She'd climbed up and down the ladder at least fifty times that morning.

"Need some help," asked a cheerful voice beneath her.

"Yes, Mom, I'm glad you're back," Lacht babbled gratefully. "Would you hand me that runaway towel?"

"We didn't need to wash windows in the Root Forest," Frenne observed as she retrieved the towel and handed it up.

"I don't mind," Lacht maintained stoutly, rubbing the dry

towel over the wet windowpane. "I love windows. I just don't like them dirty."

"They're not dirty now," stated her mother admiringly. "Everything will be clean for Lynn and Chell's visit this fall. Are you nearly through?"

"I'm done with the outside," the young woman announced, climbing down the ladder for the last time. "The inside won't take as long."

"Speaking of runaways," Frenne said, climbing the steps and sitting on the edge of the porch. "Guess what happened in town this morning?"

"What?" Lacht asked, collapsing beside her.

"We got another message about that missing girl!"

Lacht's body tensed. "What did it say?" she asked, lips closing tightly around each word.

ﬕ ﬕ ﬕ

Frenne looked sideways at her. Lacht cried easily these days, and her family never knew what would set her off. She'd started doing jobs around the cottage too—hard jobs—which, as Irsht had pointed out, was totally uncharacteristic.

"Well," the older woman answered carefully, "this message gave more particulars. A month ago, her parents found the girl exploring a dangerous part of Wasso Lake and ordered her home; but the next morning, they discovered her room empty and a sack of food gone. The Wassandra are searching the lake, but it's a large area to cover; and they wonder if she might have hidden in a cove near Burkin Village. She always wanted to see our village."

Frenne stopped talking and glanced sideways again to gauge her daughter's reaction.

"I hope they find her soon," Lacht said evenly.

"Me too," she agreed, breathing easier. "Your father is waiting at the message box along with the Burkin Village wise ones. They want to express their deep concern." She paused, then added, "Crispin and a few of his friends are watching from the shore again."

"Are they?" Lacht whispered, and her face twitched.

"Yes, they sit there and tell scary stories about the Wassandra. Then they accuse each other of being Wet Ones in disguise," Frenne said, her normally gentle voice hardened with disapproval.

Lacht's face twitched one more time before the tears gushed.

"Don't worry," Frenne told her, sorry she'd mentioned anything about Crispin. "The wise ones will handle those young people. They need to grow up a little, that's all. I'm sure they don't mean to—"

"Don't, Mom," Lacht said, lips tightening around each word again.

"Sweetling, what is it?"

"Nothing."

The young woman stood up and wiped her face. "I don't want to start the inside windows now. I'm going to take a walk. Visit Brownie."

The skin between Frenne's eyes puckered as she watched Lacht go. What on Tarth had happened to her daughter?

By the time Lacht reached the shop, she had herself under control. Nobody was in the yard, so she sat on the bottom porch step and took a deep breath. A nose nudged one of her hands.

"Well, Brownie, you came out on your own this time," she announced with surprised pleasure. "What a good brave boy!"

"Who's a good brave boy?" asked someone from inside the shop, and Ploddin limped onto the porch.

"Brownie is, yes he is," she answered, petting the brown head and crooning over the eyes raised trustingly to hers.

Ploddin snorted. "He's a timidog!" he stated loudly.

Lacht raised a scowling face, but she had to laugh when she saw the young blacksmith's grin. "Stop teasing," she told him. "Brownie's made great progress, and you know it!"

"It's phenomenal," he agreed. "I told you he follows you home every night."

"But I've never seen him do it," she complained, "and I'd love to show him off. The Root people always preferred big gray dogs with long hair. My family's never even seen a shorthaired, brown dog—I'm sure they're very rare."

"Give him more time," Ploddin suggested. "He'll come around." He made his way down the steps. "You're early today."

"Yes, I know," she remarked absently. "I'm escaping window washing."

"Ugh," he grunted and limped his way across the yard. "I finished the plow yesterday. Want to see it?"

She followed him to one side of the forge and stared silently at the twisted jumble of iron. "Does it work?" she finally asked.

"I don't know," admitted Ploddin, looking up at the sky and rubbing his chin as if in deep thought. "I'd like to check it out, but I need a yard someone wants plowed. Know of one?"

Lacht grinned. "Anytime," she said, closing her eyes and nodding fervently. "The dirt clumps in our yard deliberately harden when I walk by. I've seen them do it; I have!"

"Your mother invited Crispin and me for supper tonight," he reminded her. "Why don't I come midafternoon and make those clumps behave?"

"Yes!" she enthused, smacking one fist into the other, and Ploddin grinned at her.

"Want some lunch?" he asked next.

"Is it lunchtime?" she asked back, her face turning sunset pink. "I guess I am early."

"Go sit by the timidog," he told her. "I'll bring it out."

She watched him limp toward the cottage. "I could help," she offered.

"No," he replied without turning his head. "I may not walk

right, but I can put a sandwich together."

Lacht followed him to the porch steps, shaking her head the whole way. She'd thought they'd gotten beyond the sourplum speeches. When Brownie poked his head between two steps, she rubbed behind his ears.

"You're not an old grump, are you, Brownie?"

"I heard that," came an immediate rejoinder from inside the cottage. "Visitors who call me names get sawdust in their sandwiches."

She started to laugh, then stiffened.

Someone was coming down the road—several someones from the sound of it. Brownie's nose disappeared under the porch, and Lacht wished she could follow it. She sat on the bottom step and tried to keep her face from twitching.

Crispin and his two friends rounded a corner and shouted when they saw her.

"Lacht, you should have waited with us," Crispin called in his trumpet voice. "The Wassandra came back to the message box!"

"Well, did you see what they looked like this time?" she asked, not knowing whether to twitch or smile.

Crispin made her feel like doing both. She couldn't help but enjoy the young Stalli man's exuberance. He wore a blue shirt, open at the throat, and his dark eyes sparkled with excitement. He was definitely the handsomest man in Burkin Village.

"We didn't see anything at all," he groaned. "The wise ones wouldn't let us on the pier, and the Wassandra didn't come out of the water again."

Ploddin stumped his way outside with a tray of sandwiches, and Crispin cheered loudly. He took the tray from his brother, passing it around to everyone, as if personally responsible for each and every sandwich.

"Take all you want," he urged them generously. "There's more where these came from."

Lacht glanced at Ploddin. Did he ever resent his brother's ways?

Ploddin had taken a sandwich to one of the porch chairs. He didn't look sour exactly, just resigned.

"Ploddin, are there any more sandwiches?" one of the young men had the nerve to ask.

"Fixings are in the kitchen," he answered, his body settling deeper into the chair, and his face losing the resigned look as it puckered into familiar lines.

"I make the best sandwiches in Stalli," boasted Crispin, hand flourishing high in the air. "Come on, I'll show you how."

Crispin and his friends rushed up the steps and into the cottage, but Lacht stayed in the yard.

Ploddin glanced at her.

"I'm sorry," she murmured. "I don't think he means—"

"I know," he interrupted. "He doesn't."

Neither of them had anything further to say. They finished eating their sandwiches, then Ploddin pushed himself up and brushed off some stray crumbs.

"Something to drink?" he asked.

Lacht opened her mouth, but before she could respond, Crispin, followed by his friends, came outside carrying a tray filled with steaming cups.

"I made tea," he said. "You have to boil the water, steep the tea leaves for exactly two minutes, then add a dollop of honey. Here you go. Have a cup of the best tea in Stalli!"

Lacht thanked him as she took a cup. Ploddin just took a cup.

"We're going swimming this afternoon," Crispin announced enthusiastically. "A little cove south of town gets full sun for several hours. You two should go with us! Lacht, it's quite safe in the cove area, and we'll stay beside you every minute. Ploddin, you work too hard. I'd like to see you have fun every now and then."

Lacht jumped up, shaking her head. "I can't, I have to go home," she said, her words jerking like hammer strokes. "I—Mom—they need me," she finished and took three steps before realizing one hand still held the cup of tea.

"Here," she said, pushing the cup at Crispin and sloshing hot tea all over her hand.

"It's quite—" he started to repeat, but Ploddin interrupted him.

"Leave her alone," he said, and his mouth twisted as if he'd eaten a dozen sourplums, one after another. "Let her go."

Lacht's face flushed brighter than a sunset this time. She turned away before they could see her tears.

"But," Crispin began, arms going out to either side in bewilderment.

"Let her go," snapped his brother again.

Crispin shook his head and went back into the cottage. Through narrowed eyes, Ploddin watched Lacht go around the corner. He kept looking. Sure enough, a little brown tail whisked across the road after her.

♫ ♫ ♫

"It works!" marveled Lacht later that afternoon.

"Of course, it works," Ploddin responded, nose rising to a how-could-you-doubt-me level as he surveyed the front yard.

The plow certainly did work. Lacht stared wide-eyed at the hours of work accomplished in minutes.

"Do the rest of it," she ordered happily, "sides and back."

The young man stared at her. His forehead lifted a little too dramatically for real crossness. "Easy for you to say."

"You're getting supper," she said, trying to stare him down. "You might as well work for it."

His gaze shifted up to the violet sky. He rubbed his chin thoughtfully, and she changed tactics.

"Mom made blueberry pie and whipped cream for dessert," she coaxed with a sideways tilt of her head toward the kitchen.

"Blueberry pie!" he repeated, his gaze dropping swiftly. "That's good. That's very good. What else?"

"We finally had our well cleaned today," Lacht answered

brightly. "I'm tired of boiling all the water we need. Tonight we'll have fresh, cold water straight from the well."

Ploddin's face turned blank.

"Oh yes," she said, hiding a smile at his lack of interest in fresh, cold water. "We're having a roast with potatoes and carrots and onions. Mom will probably make biscuits too, and we'll have butter and honey."

"Biscuits!" he said so loudly that there was no doubt he and Crispin were indeed brothers. "Why didn't you say so?"

He turned the plow and started on one of the side yards, while she ran up the porch steps and into the big Stalli kitchen.

"Mom, you're making biscuits for supper, aren't you?" she asked breathlessly. "We need lots of them."

"We heard," answered her mother with a laugh.

Winnel, busy cutting up carrots at the counter, laughed too.

"Better make a double batch," he advised.

Aromas from the roast were wafting out the kitchen windows by the time Ploddin finished plowing. He sniffed appreciatively as he stumbled over to the porch where Lacht sat. Silently, she watched him come. All the plowing had made his limp worse, but she knew better than to say anything.

"If Keshua had made a flower smell like that," he announced as he eased himself into the rocking chair next to her, "I'd plant a flower bed!"

"It'd make you hungry all the time," she disagreed mildly, still feeling bad about his limp.

They rocked together for a few minutes, then he leaned forward and whispered, "There," as he pointed to a neighbor's row of bushes.

Lacht stared in the direction he'd pointed, but she couldn't see a thing except for blue leaves.

"No, he's gone again," Ploddin said, settling back into the chair. "He saw me pointing. That dog can melt into the ground. The dark color of the dirt helps camouflage him, of course; which is why Brownie likes to sneak around under bushes where no grass grows."

Lacht quit trying to stare through leaves and stared at Ploddin instead. She sniffed and her nose rose to a how-could-you level.

He visibly braced himself.

"If he'd had green hair, you would have named him Greenie," she told him accusingly. "If he'd had blue hair, he would have been Bluey, and if he'd had gray hair, but no, some things are better left unsaid. Anyway," she finished, glancing back in the direction of the bushes, "I'm not convinced you really saw him."

Ploddin opened his mouth to defend himself, but Irsht came up one road and Crispin down another, and the conversation ended.

Seven

Well Water

"This is delicious," Crispin told Frenne thirty minutes later as he reached for the big dish of roast in the middle of the table.

"I'm glad you—" his hostess started to say, but the unfortunate bump of Crispin's hand against Lacht's water glass stopped her.

Water spilled from the overturned glass, ran swiftly across the table, and fell into the Stalli girl's lap. Everyone except for her tried to grab the glass at the same time.

"Lacht, I'm sorry," Crispin kept saying; but she was staring fixedly down at her lap and didn't hear him.

Her legs felt wet underneath her dress, soggy wet, and the cold, damp feeling of material clinging to skin was the most delightful thing that had ever happened to her.

Wasso Lake water became normal water when it was boiled. Crispin had told them that long ago. But this water was—*straight from the well and not boiled; and I'm wet everywhere the water fell on me! I'm equally wet everywhere—no strange dry places. Surely that means—.*

She laughed out loud.

"I'm sorry, Lacht," Crispin said again.

This time she heard him. "It's nothing, Crispin. I'll go change. Don't let anybody eat my piece of pie," she said with such lighthearted abandon that she felt a little faint.

Beaming the whole way down the hall to her bedroom, she whipped off her wet things and put on dry ones.

It wasn't true all along, she sang to herself. *I must have imagined it. Irsht is right. I have too much imagination. I'm wet; oh, I'm wet! I'm so very, very wet!*

A few minutes later, she returned to the table, still beaming. Everyone smiled back except for Ploddin, who sat very still, staring at her; staring hard, with an odd look on his face.

When it was time for dessert, Frenne put an enormous pie plate on the table and served large pieces of pie, topped with hand-whipped cream. Crispin and Ploddin took their first bites and then sat back, half closing their eyes, reveling in the wonderful mixture of blueberries and custard.

Yes, you can tell they're brothers, thought Lacht happily as she munched on her own big bite.

Winnel opened his mouth to compliment his wife on her culinary masterpiece, but Irsht spoke before he could.

"Can I have another piece?" she asked feverishly.

"You've barely started that one!" her mother answered, scandalized at the question.

"Yes, I know," agreed the indomitable young woman, "but I asked first, before anyone else. Remember that!"

Frenne shook her head at her youngest daughter, while Lacht and Winnel broke into peals of laughter.

"You two don't know the epic love story entitled, 'Irsht Meets Blueberries,'" Lacht told Crispin and Ploddin.

She hadn't talked this freely in days. Eyes shining and hands gesturing in the air, she explained the background to her story.

"Enormous blueberry bushes grew in the Root Forest wherever enough sunlight came through the trees. The blueberries got almost as big as our Root neighbors' eyes!"

"Heavy dews provided daily moisture," Winnel added. "All the bushes needed was sunlight."

Lacht nodded and continued, "Not long after we first arrived at the forest, Irsht ran away."

"Did not!" her sister placidly interrupted, stuffing another bite of pie into her mouth.

"Well, we thought she'd run away. Mom and Dad refused to consider the possibility of kidnapping, but I thought differently. Root Forest people, with their large heads and hands, seemed very strange to me. I felt certain they'd taken my sister and were out to get me."

"Lacht stayed with us the whole time we searched for Irsht. Everyone was impressed. I hugged her over and over for loving her little sister that much," Frenne added with a chuckle.

"I wasn't about to leave you," Lacht agreed cheerfully. "I knew they'd get me too, if I did. When we finally found Irsht, she was sitting under a big blueberry bush with three Root children, all of them stuffing in blueberries faster than a scared timidog can run."

"It was a contest," Irsht remarked. "I won."

"From then on, Irsht has loved blueberries. In every other respect, she is calm and practical, but if she sees a blueberry bush—get out of her way!"

"All done," announced Irsht smugly. "Mom?"

"Our guests," protested Frenne weakly as Crispin and Ploddin roared with laughter.

"Divide what's left into thirds," Irsht advised her mother. "Give one third to each boy and one to me. You and Dad and Lacht never take a second piece anyway."

Frenne shook her head once more but obediently divided up the remainder of the pie.

"I'll take that one," ordered Irsht, pointing toward the biggest piece.

"They are equal in size," her mother responded firmly, a warning glint in her eye, "or they will be once I serve them."

Irsht lowered her head, accepting the reproof. She also accepted her second serving of pie.

"Hurry up, Ploddin," she said then, examining his plate. "Crispin's way ahead of you."

"Ploddin never could eat as quickly as I could," Crispin bragged. "Our parents said I lifted a fork faster than anyone else in Stalli."

"Well," Lacht stated in Ploddin's defense, "he lifts a tool faster!"

"And much more often," Ploddin dryly commented.

Crispin grinned as the whole family laughed at him. "I have important things to do, bringing in new customers and keeping old ones. We have a partnership, see!"

When Ploddin shook his head at his brother, the expression so resembled Frenne's face when she'd shaken her head at Irsht that Lacht laughed out loud again.

"If I didn't know better," Crispin said, lifting up his water glass and inspecting its contents carefully, "I would think you'd given us well water mixed with water from Wasso Lake. Outbreaks of hysterical laughter, entirely unprovoked, result from drinking that water, I've always heard."

"Nobody drinks Wasso Lake water," Frenne answered in amusement. "We got this water from our well."

"But the water's all, uh, connected," broke in Lacht, staring back and forth between Crispin and her mother. "I mean, I know our well water's green, not gold, but water from the lake must mix in with it."

"Most streams flow into Wasso Lake and turn golden when they get there. Only a few flow out," Crispin informed her, "and they leave from the other side of the lake. The outgoing streams stay gold a couple of miles before they become green again. People say jostling over rocks is what changes the color back, but we don't really know."

"You can't tell what's going on underground." Lacht argued the only point that interested her; her fists clenched into tight balls under the table. "Our well water must have Wasso Lake water in it. We're too close to the lake!"

"Not a chance," he corrected her, nodding his thanks as Frenne served him his second piece of pie. "We'd know by the color. Gold dominates over green. Stallis have experimented, you know. I did it myself once. A half cup of water from Wasso Lake made a whole bucketful of well water golden. We have the most mysterious lake in all of Stalli," he boasted with his trademark hand flourish.

Lacht didn't want to give up. "You can't know what goes on underground," she repeated insistently, though her voice had started shaking. "Our well probably has a trace of golden water in it, not enough to affect the color, but enough to, uh, be there."

"Not a drop," Crispin informed her without hesitation. "We never drink out of Wasso Lake. Who knows what the Wassandra's water might do to us!"

"How close are you to working on our table and chairs?" asked Winnel, in an obvious effort to change the subject.

Ploddin answered, and the ensuing conversation circled around Lacht as if the words were a whirlpool, only she couldn't get sucked into them because she was already drowning at the bottom. She stared at her empty plate silently. She must have finished her piece of pie without noticing.

What a waste, she thought dully.

"Lacht, supper is over," Frenne said.

She lifted her head. Crispin and Irsht stood laughing over something at the door; Winnel had carried an armload of dishes to the sink; and Frenne was stacking her own armload.

Ploddin stood by his chair, staring intently at her again.

"Come sit on the porch with me," he said.

Her body felt too heavy to move, but if she stayed at the table, someone would ask why. She got up and walked outside.

Ploddin sat and motioned to the chair next to him. She made herself sit in it.

"We're going to watch the nightlights above Wasso Lake," called Irsht from the darkening street. "Come on, you two!"

"No thanks," Ploddin called back firmly. "We'll stay here."

Lacht didn't answer. Ploddin glanced at her, but she didn't turn her head in his direction. She couldn't. Her head weighed too much to turn.

"I know," he stated abruptly, "that you are a Wet One."

She didn't know how anything that heavy could move so quickly, but one moment she sat in the chair, and the next she leaned on the porch railing as far from Ploddin as she could get. She didn't say anything. She just leaned over the railing, and the knuckles on her hands whitened as she clutched at the wood.

"When the water spilled on your lap, I suspected it," he said next, staring at her. "I suspected it because not long after my accident, well water sloshed against my arm, and I felt released, free, full of explosive joy. Born and raised in Burkin Village, I should have known better, but I was young and I didn't understand the makeup of well water. When I found out that the water that had wet my arm didn't come from Wasso Lake, I wanted to die. I saw your face when you found out the same thing tonight. That's when I knew."

He leaned back in his chair as if surely he'd said enough. However, Lacht stayed by the railing, her breathing coming in short gasps. Ploddin made one more statement, though it sounded as if he had to force each of these words out of his mouth.

"I know that you're a Wet One, Lacht, because I'm a Wet One too!"

She was off the porch and running before he'd finished talking. She heard him call her name and begin stomping down the steps, but she didn't stop. He'd never catch up with her, not with his limp.

Cutting across three yards, Lacht bolted down a road. When

she reached a corner, she turned away from the center of the village and kept running. She turned again twice. The last road ended in woods, and she hesitated only briefly before plunging into the quiet of the trees.

The quiet comforted her. She sniffed at the leaves and bark around her almost hungrily. The woodsy smell reminded her of the Root Forest, and that comforted her too. She slowed down to a walk.

This time she expected the sudden descent of the ground. Sitting on the top of the short cliff, just as she'd sat the first time she saw Wasso Lake, she stared at the moving mists beneath her. Overhead, nightlights lit the golden hues as if lighting a candle, a giant swirling candle.

Her heart pounded, and her muscles convulsed, but the mists swirled and danced with carefree abandon.

"I was right," she finally whispered. "They are beautiful."

Without giving herself any more time to think, she grasped her skirt firmly on either side and slid down the steep cliff. Her skirt would get dirty this way, but she wouldn't have to add a fall to an already catastrophic evening.

The strategy worked well.

In fact, she slid further than she meant to, and the golden mists swirled up to her waist before she could stop. She breathed in sharply, but nothing happened. Mists pirouetted about her legs, and she inched down a little more. She wanted to get to the water, but she'd have to go all the way into the mists to do that.

Slowly, Lacht entered a golden world. She kept sliding until she could see the water, a solid pane of gold. The mists danced a few feet above the smooth surface.

Go on.

She forced herself to put both feet into the water. Sand supported the bottoms of her shoes firmly enough, but she couldn't feel the water, even when it rose above her ankles, and she could see it on the calves of her legs.

Tears gathered in the corners of her eyes, then slid down her cheeks as smoothly as she was sliding down into Wasso Lake. Down and down, until the water covered her head, and she closed her eyes and held her breath involuntarily.

Try it. Maybe it won't work.

She let air out through her mouth. Then she breathed back in, eyes tightly closed, hoping hard to gag. Again, nothing happened. She couldn't feel any water in her mouth or nose. As far as she could tell, her body was breathing normally—in and out, in and out.

One eye opened, then the other one, and she looked across the slowly descending bottom of the lake. Perhaps the strange gold color of the water produced a light of its own; perhaps the water absorbed light from the bright mists swirling above it; but, in any case, Lacht could see under the surface of Wasso Lake.

She remembered swimming with Irsht in Root Forest ponds. Whenever she'd opened her eyes under those ponds, she'd felt the pressure of water pushing into them. Now her eyes felt normal. She blinked to see how that felt, and the blink felt normal too.

On and on in front of her, the sand sloped gently downwards. It must have eventually leveled off, but she couldn't tell where the slope ended and level ground began. She sat where she had stopped in her downward slide and stared at the golden slope in front of her. Occasionally, she lifted her eyes to the misty shimmer overhead.

When she finally turned and crawled out of Wasso Lake, Lacht was no longer crying. She crawled up the steep bank and stood at its top, brushing dirt off her skirt and marveling in a detached way at the dry material.

Slowly, she walked through the trees and followed the roads of Burkin Village back to her cottage, still feeling detached; as if she were looking at a young woman walking beside her; a young woman who had accepted the fact that she was a Wet One.

Nobody at home asked where she had been. Lacht assumed that Ploddin had left quietly. Her family all thought she'd taken a walk with him.

She got ready for bed, answering Irsht's chatter with a minimum of words. Finally, she lay under the covers, listening to her sister breathe and staring through the window at the colorful nightlights of the Tarth sky.

What would her family think? She pictured their responses inside her mind and found herself smiling.

Irsht would promptly and completely change her mind about Wet Ones. She'd reject Crispin's descriptions with a lifted nose and a matter-of-fact, "Of course, Wet Ones don't have pale skin and webbed feet. They never did! People just enjoy letting their imaginations fly. I've always said so."

Frenne's face would wrinkle anxiously at first, but she'd remember her grandmother's stories. Once she got over the initial worry, she'd thrill to the thought. "A Wet One, what an honor!" she'd insist.

However, it was the calm, steady words Lacht imagined Winnel saying that put a yawn in her mouth and a droop on her eyelids. "Keshua created you. He sent the Plete to live inside you, and the Plete gave you gifts to use for other people, just as he gives gifts to everyone. The Plete does not make mistakes!"

She was a Wet One, but she was still loved. She was a Wet One because Keshua had made her that way. She was...her eyes closed as she fell into a peaceful sleep.

Eight

The Last Dream

This dream began differently. Lacht wasn't standing in the middle of long, red leaves. The sun shone directly above her, and she was flying, not standing. She couldn't see leaves at all.

Wait, that wasn't true. Leaves fluttered below her, lots of leaves, but they were small leaves this time, forming a fluttering, blue coverlet that rose and fell as it encountered mountains and valleys and ridges and gullies and small curves of land that didn't have a name.

When autumn arrived, she knew the coverlet would turn purple, with pink spots here or there, wherever fruit and nut trees grew. Crispin had told her that fall in the Stalli Mountains was more beautiful than anywhere else on Tarth.

She soared high above the mountain leaves and delighted in the clear air and expansive view.

It's wonderful, Keshua.

A glimmer of gold in the distance announced the approach of Wasso Lake. As Lacht flew closer, what she could see of the lake expanded until the golden surface, quivering with its submerged, noontime mists, dominated the landscape.

She looked at it with a smile. After all, Keshua had created Wasso Lake too. The gold water and mists belonged in Tarth, just like the blue-leafed trees and the purple sky and that golden waterfall beneath her.

The small waterfall cascaded out of the lake over a big rock and dashed away between the trees. She flew above the stream, enjoying its boldness and vigor. Looking ahead, she could see where it emptied into a pond, a golden pond that quivered with its own submerged mists.

She was coming down now. Lacht landed on the edge of the water and studied the pond. She couldn't see very far below its surface, of course; but, on one side, there was a wide circle of gold that looked thicker than the rest. Sticks, or maybe branches, curved above the water within the circle.

Her skin prickled. She swallowed convulsively as she stared, unable to move her eyes away.

Then her body moved again, walking to the edge of the pond and into the water. She didn't want to go. She tried to hold back and would have screamed if she could have, but it was a dream and she was not the one in charge of it.

Down she went into golden water for the second time that night. She clutched at a cone-shaped rock with one hand and a tall cluster of blue, water reeds with the other, but the effort to stop didn't work. She couldn't get a good grip on the rock, and the reeds wrenched loose from her hand as her body moved steadily down. Down, until the waters of the pond closed over her head, and she couldn't see the outside world any longer.

The ground dropped very steeply to the bottom of the pond, but her dream didn't let her fall. Walking quickly, albeit reluctantly, she reached level ground and cringed away from a cavern of darkness on her left.

She didn't want to go into that darkness, and this time her dream agreed with her. Turning to the right, she hurried into long, purple things that twisted around her.

The leaves from my other dreams, she realized suddenly, *only they're not red now. Autumn must come earlier here than it does above the water.*

There was no more time to think. Fear knifed its way into her from something that lurched out of the cavern of darkness behind her. Lacht's mind screamed loudly even if her mouth couldn't make a sound. With a rush, she went deeper into the flowing purple leaves, and the something halted outside of them.

She gasped a half-sob of relief. The fear knives could come through the leaves, but whatever had thrown them couldn't. Moving rapidly forward, she reached the cave in the middle of the leaves.

A small figure crouched in a tight ball on the floor of the cave. Only a dim light seeped through the surrounding leaves; nevertheless, she could see the Wassandra girl much more clearly in this dream. Reed-thin arms wrapped themselves around legs not much bigger than the ropes Winnel made.

She looks younger than eleven, Lacht thought, and her eyes softened. *What will she do when the leaves fall? That scary thing will come then. It will come and get her.*

As if in direct response to the thought, her body spun around and ran out of the cave, back through the leaves. She didn't have time to scream, however silently, before she faced for one stilled heartbeat what stood outside the leaves on two stubby legs.

The creature couldn't see her, which was a comfort. However, she could see it, and Lacht found no comfort in that at all.

Above the stubby legs, a short trunk rose, its dull orange color clashing unpleasantly with the golden water. Five snaky arms wiggled and groped fifteen feet beyond their body. A round head without a neck stared out of lidless eyes.

The mouth opened, and an orange tongue licked its lips.

Lacht screamed her loudest silent scream yet, then gasped another half-sob of relief as her body left the monster and rushed upwards. With a burst of golden bubbles, she broke the surface of the pond and continued rising, high into the air.

Heart racing and breath hyperventilating, she glanced downwards and saw the stream. From that height, it resembled a line someone had drawn with a pencil, a golden line that traveled from the pond to the waterfall. Her face lifted a little further, and she saw Burkin Village on the other side of the lake....

Eyes starting open, Lacht stared into the darkness of her room. Irsht turned over in the bed next to her.

"Only another dream," Lacht started to whisper, but the words stuck in her throat.

The next morning, Lacht slouched into the kitchen and growled at her mother. At least, Frenne thought her older daughter had growled. Maybe the growl had contained words.

"Did you sleep well?" she asked.

"No," snapped Lacht. "May I have some tea?"

Frenne poured a cup of tea and pushed the honey within reach. She didn't dare ask if Lacht wanted honey. Her daughter's expression indicated she needed sweetening, but the girl ignored the honey. She didn't even drink the tea. She just stared into the steam rising from her cup.

When Winnel and Irsht arrived, she ignored them too, though she did raise the cup and take a sip. Her daughter's sour face reminded Frenne of someone. *Oh yes...*

"I think Ploddin and Crispin had a good time last night, don't you?" she asked her family brightly.

"Definitely," answered Irsht, while Winnel nodded and smiled.

Lacht resumed staring into her cup. She had decided to talk to Ploddin that morning. He was the only one she wanted to talk to, however. She wasn't accepting her Wet One status as graciously this morning as she had last night, and she didn't want her family to know.

They'd support her. Oh yes, they'd support her. She could still picture in her mind how each member of her family would leap lovingly to her side. The very thought of those loving leaps gave her a headache.

She glared into her cup.

"Let's talk to the Great One after breakfast," Winnel suggested when he'd finished his oatmeal. "We'll ask him again to direct the Wassandra to their missing girl."

"He should have done it before now," Lacht complained, and her father raised his eyebrows. "It's been weeks," she growled defensively. "Her parents have suffered, everyone who's exhausted themselves searching for her has suffered, and the girl herself has suffered."

"We don't know about the girl," pointed out Irsht. "She might be having fun!"

"She is not having fun," stated Lacht and glared across the table. "I know."

"Oh, you had another dream, didn't you!" her sister announced rather than asked. "That explains your bad mood."

Lacht opened her mouth quickly, but before she could speak, Winnel intervened.

"That's enough, girls," he said.

Their father didn't often use that tone. Both girls dropped their eyes and stared at their plates.

"Lacht," Winnel said next, "you're wondering why the Great One hasn't done anything."

"We've asked him," she mumbled. "Lots of people have asked him. The girl's still gone."

"He heard us," he insisted, leaning back in his chair, "all of us, and he answered each request."

"We asked him to return the girl to her parents, and she's still missing," she said, still staring at her plate. "Maybe we should have asked Keshua instead."

"You know better than that," Frenne said, sounding surprised. "Keshua is the Great One's son. They answer the same."

Maybe her mother had raised her eyebrows too. Lacht didn't

know. She refused to look up.

"Situations are more complicated than we can possibly understand," Winnel pointed out, "with a lot of people involved. Perhaps the Great One's working good in the hearts of her parents, perhaps in the hearts of those searching for her, perhaps in the heart of the girl herself. Who knows, he might send someone to her this very day!"

Lacht finally raised her head but didn't say anything. She went with the others into the small sitting room after breakfast and listened while they asked the Great One for help. Irsht addressed her prayer rather pointedly to Keshua. Frenne talked about the Plete guiding them.

Still, Lacht didn't say anything.

Lacht worked listlessly on the yard until midmorning. Then she dragged herself through the village to Ploddin's cottage, where she found the young blacksmith building up the fire in his outdoors forge.

He didn't look at her. Throwing a bucketful of coal into the fire, he encouraged the flames with an old bellows that blew as much coal dust into the yard as it blew air into the fire.

"You need a new bellows," she informed him.

Lacht had hoped her bad mood would go away as she walked. It hadn't.

Ploddin didn't respond. He bent over the forge, pumping mightily with the old bellows for several more minutes. Then he threw in another bucket of coal, squinted into the fire again, straightened up, and scowled at her.

She scowled back. They traded scowls for a full minute before he limped to his chair and picked up his hammer.

"Where did you go last night?" he asked gruffly.

She hesitated, glancing at the cottage door.

"Crispin's not home," he told her, his gruffness easing slightly.

She faced him and took a deep breath. "I went to Wasso Lake to see if it was true. It is. I'm a Wet One."

"What did you do?" he asked, narrowing his eyes.

"The only thing I could do," she whispered. "I went under the lake."

"You could have gotten hurt!" he immediately snapped, slamming his hammer onto the workbench so hard that she jumped.

"Don't be silly," she snapped back. "I breathed underwater. When I came out, my clothes were dry. So now I know."

"Don't ever do that again," he commanded, intensifying his scowl and adding to it a touch of worried concern.

It was the concern that kept her from leaving. Her scowl deepened, but she didn't leave.

"No one knows what's under Wasso Lake," he stated next. "It's a dangerous place."

"I think you've listened too long to Crispin's stories," Lacht told him. "I didn't see anything—" Midsentence, she remembered her dream of the night before, and her voice trailed off.

"You've lived in Burkin Village for two weeks," he reminded her. "I've lived here all my life."

"Ploddin, when did you find out you were a Wet One?" she asked, making an immense effort to change the tone of their conversation.

Dropping his hammer, the young man slowly brushed coal dust from his hands as he prepared to tell the story he'd kept secret for twenty long years. Opening his mouth, he closed it before any words could come out. Then he tried again, with the same result.

"When I turned four, I followed Crispin and some of the older boys to the lake," he finally managed to say.

"They wanted to go swimming and, for the first time, I had permission to go with them, though my parents said I could only wade. The big boys jumped in and splashed and yelled, while water ran off their wet hair. I tried to kick up enough water to make my hair wet too, but I lost my balance and sat down. It didn't matter. This would get me wet too. I lay back and dipped my hair into the water, but when I lifted my head—"

"I know," Lacht said gently when he paused, his face contorted with a twenty-year-old pain. "Nothing was wet."

"I'd heard the stories," he continued, his words coming quicker now. "Wet Ones were crazy people, misfits, monsters. I jumped up from the water that refused to drip from my clothes and ran towards home, too scared to cry. When a boulder got in my way, I scrambled up it, fell, and broke my leg. Then I made the break worse trying to pull myself away from the lake. Crispin heard my screams and carried me home. I've never gone near Wasso Lake since." He stopped talking to wipe sweat from his forehead.

"Didn't you ever—" she began to ask.

"No," he answered shortly.

"I mean, wasn't something in you attracted to—"

"No!"

She puckered one side of her mouth. "Honestly, Ploddin, I'm sorry you broke your leg, but that happened because you panicked and ran, not because Wasso Lake was out to get you. The Plete made us Wet Ones, and we're supposed to use his gifts for the good of other people."

"That sounds like something your father would say," Ploddin scoffed.

Lacht spun around, stomped to the porch, and sat on its bottom step. She didn't say anything; she merely glared at Ploddin. When a brown nose pushed between her arm and side, she patted its accompanying head without looking at it.

The yard stayed quiet a few minutes. Checking the heat in his forge again, the young blacksmith added more coal, making the warmth from the fire reach all the way across the yard. It felt good. Lacht watched Ploddin until he turned and looked in her direction.

He smiled halfheartedly. "I didn't say it was bad to sound like your father."

"You implied it," she said, but her face relaxed. She even managed a half-smile.

He walked over and sat next to her on the step. To her surprise, Brownie immediately pushed a snuffling nose against him. Patting the little head, he glanced sideways at Lacht. "You aren't the only one dogs like, you know."

She nodded. "Ploddin?"

He waited. When she didn't say anything further, he tried to help her out. "Yes?"

"Have you ever had dreams?"

Ploddin cleared his throat. The one thing he could say with certainty about Lacht was that she was unpredictable. "Everyone dreams."

"I've had dreams," she told him abruptly, "about that Wassandra girl. I want to tell you about them."

There, she'd said it!

He shrugged. "All right, go ahead."

"Well," she began, suddenly in a hurry. "I've dreamed about the missing girl four times now. She's trapped under the water, with long red leaves surrounding her. Each dream got a little more focused, until I could see that the leaves have turned purple. They're about to fall. That wouldn't matter except that they protect the girl from a horrible water monster. I saw it last night at the end of my last dream," she said with a shudder. "It's orange with snaky arms and no neck and eyes without eyelids. As soon as the leaves drop, it'll get her. The girl keeps crying out for help. I've got to go to her."

Not until then, as she voiced those last words, did Lacht know what the Plete wanted her to do.

Unfortunately, Ploddin did not appear to have received the same revelation. "Irsht will teach in the village school this fall, right?" he asked sharply.

She shrugged. "Yes, but I don't understand what—"

"She's brought home books that she plans to use with the

younger children, hasn't she? Books with pictures and stories in them?"

Lacht stared at him. "I really don't—"

"You've just described to me a picture from one of those books, the picture of an underwater creature. I remember the picture clearly because it frightened me as a child. Do you remember the creature's name? You must have seen its name written in capital letters above the picture."

"Ploddin, I haven't seen that picture."

"I think you have," he insisted. "You may not remember, but you've seen it and then dreamed about it. The creature's called a Wert and has five long arms coming out of its body with dagger-like nails on the ends of its fingers. It eats fish, but a Wert is always hungry and will eat anything else that comes its way. It throws out an aura of fear to paralyze its victims. Then it walks up to them, and they can't move because its lidless eyes hypnotize them. The last thing they see is a mouth, open wide—"

"Stop!" she screamed, jumping to her feet.

The vivid description had brought back all the horror of the creature in her dream, only now the creature had a name.

Ploddin jumped up too. He grabbed her by the shoulders and shook her. "Lacht, calm down. You had a nightmare brought on by that picture. Believe me, I know. I dreamed about it too, years ago. I've never liked the color, orange, since."

She focused on his face and tried to sound coherent. "I don't know that monster from a book; I know it from my last dream."

He released her shoulders abruptly and stared at her.

"Keshua gave me those dreams for a reason," she continued. "He wants us to—"

"You can leave out the 'us' part," he interrupted. "I didn't have any dreams from Keshua, and I don't think you did either. You just saw that picture in one of Irsht's books."

Lacht wrung her hands together. Now that she knew what Keshua wanted her to do, she had a strong awareness of time passing—crucial time. "The leaves have turned purple.... They're about to fall."

"Well," he replied, maddeningly calm, "that's another thing that proves you saw the picture. The caption beneath it explains that the long leaves of a panotka plant contain a substance that chokes off a Wert's air supply—or whatever underwater monsters breathe in that disgusting lake. You can see why I don't want you in the water! Dangerous things live there. We don't know much about them."

"I know all I need to know," she told him, breathing fast. "Won't you come with me, Ploddin? I'd feel much better if you came with me."

"You're crazy," he sputtered. "I haven't gone near Wasso Lake in twenty years. You've lived in Burkin Village for two weeks, only two weeks; and now you want to march into Wasso Lake and impress everyone. What could you do that the Wassandra haven't done? You don't even know where to start looking, do you?"

"As a matter of fact, I do," she shouted, completely losing her temper. "The Plete showed me where the girl is; she's not in Wasso Lake; and I do NOT want to impress everyone! What a nasty thing to say! Maybe all I can do for that Wassandra girl is keep her company, but at least that's something. I'm not going to stay here and ignore her cries for help."

Lacht's glare at Ploddin could only be matched by his glare at her. He opened his mouth, but she hadn't finished.

"I've lived in Burkin Village for only two weeks. You're right about that. I've lived in a self-centered cocoon of fear that someone would find out I'm a Wet One for two long weeks. You've lived that way for twenty years. I guess I can't expect anything from you. Your cocoon is too thick!"

"Hey, come back here," shouted Ploddin as Lacht ran out of the yard.

He tried to run after her, but his bad leg twisted, throwing him hard on the ground. He lifted his head as soon as he could and stared desperately around, but Lacht had already passed out of sight.

Nine

To the Pond

L acht ran through Burkin Village until she had to stop and hang wheezing over the gate of someone's yard. She'd made it to the edge of town that bordered the forest, but this frenzied kind of traveling had to end. She couldn't run all the way around Wasso Lake.

What she needed to do was walk at a fast, steady pace until she reached the waterfall from her dream, the one that poured over a big rock and became a stream. She'd follow the stream until it ended in the golden pond. Then—but she didn't want to think that far ahead.

"Get there first," she told herself.

Several roads ended in woods on this side of Burkin Village. She'd never walked to the end of this particular road, but there wouldn't be any problem finding the lake. The ground sloped generally downwards until it reached the water.

As soon as her breathing slowed from a wheeze to a pant, she pushed herself off the gate, but she didn't leave, not yet. The gate led into a yard, and right inside the yard sat a well, a well with a bright yellow cup dangling on a hook. The cup shone as if someone had just washed it.

Running hard on a warm summer's day has a tendency to make a person thirsty, even in the mountains.

Besides, Lacht hadn't had anything to drink since breakfast. Her clothes were sticking to her skin, and her lips had gone dry.

Making up her mind suddenly, she opened the gate and hurried toward the well.

"Hello there," a cheerful call came from the cottage behind the well. "Are you hungry?"

Lacht jumped. She didn't have time to talk.

"Hold on," the call continued. "I just made cinnamon rolls. They're perfect right after they come out of the oven, and I need you to eat one and tell me how good it is. I can't do it myself because I'm trying to lose weight, so I need you to do it for me, see?"

The woman who waddled out of the cottage door with a large cinnamon roll in her hand was definitely overweight. Rolls of fat hid her neck and bounced when she walked, but Lacht liked the twinkle in her eyes. The woman talked so much that Lacht didn't have to explain herself, and she liked that even better.

"My husband enjoys a fresh cinnamon roll, but he's not home. If I can't eat them, at least I can smell them, but it's better to see someone eat one, and, as I said, they're at their best right after I take them out of the oven. There now, take a bite and tell me it's good. That'll satisfy me!"

She thrust the large roll at the girl, whose mouth was watering enough by now to compete with the waterfall she meant to find.

Cinnamon rolls ranked high on Lacht's list of favorite treats, right up there with the famous Stalli sweet rolls. The aroma of this particular roll, liberally stuffed with cinnamon, butter, and sugar all toasted and melted together, had invaded her nose as soon as the woman opened the door.

I won't take long, she informed herself hastily and took a bite. "Ummm," she moaned in honest appreciation. "I've never had a more delicious cinnamon roll," she told the woman standing expectantly before her.

"Wait till Hanri hears that!" she chortled. "He loves it when people compliment my cooking. Well, I'll get back to the kitchen. The worst part of cooking is cleaning up!"

She waddled happily back to her kitchen door, as Lacht finished devouring the big, fluffy roll and took a long drink of water.

"Thanks, Keshua," she muttered, closing the gate on her way out of the yard. "I needed that."

Leaving the road, Lacht plunged into the trees with a feeling of relief. It wasn't likely that she'd run into anyone else, not inside the forest. In minutes, she had reached the edge of the bank that overhung Wasso Lake and started walking beside it.

Two hours later, the sun shone directly overhead and she still walked beside Wasso Lake, feeling frustrated with the density of the trees. She couldn't walk fast when she had to push her way through branches. Fortunately, the trees thinned out ahead.

As soon as possible, Lacht picked up her pace, but another twenty minutes passed before she heard the unmistakable sound of splashing water.

"At last," she said out loud, scurrying around a bush.

The golden water in front of her ran down its big rock to form a stream, a stream that said, "Hurry up," as it dashed away through the woods.

Lacht stood only a minute gazing at the rock. She hadn't meant to stop at all, but the cascade of water was unexpectedly beautiful. Sunlight poured through an opening in the trees and made the golden drops shine as if they were part water, part light.

She couldn't stay.

"Hurry up!" the current said over and over, leading the way through the trees. She turned from the rock and obediently hurried.

If I make it through this day, I'll come back, she promised herself. *I'll bring a whole basketful of cinnamon rolls and have a picnic.*

According to Crispin, the streams flowing out of Wasso Lake didn't go far before they turned into normal green water. Did he say one mile or two?

"I hope it's not three!"

She hurried, slowed to catch her breath, then hurried again, licking lips that had gone dry for the second time that morning and stealing glances at the stream.

Crispin had said Stallis shouldn't drink the golden water; but then that young man had said lots of things about Wasso Lake, and all of them were certainly not true.

Yet her mother had agreed with him on that point, Lacht remembered with a grimace.

However, Stallis had undoubtedly developed prejudices towards the lake over the years. Maybe they could drink the golden water and didn't know it. Maybe Wet Ones could drink from Wasso Lake even if other Stallis couldn't.

Licking her lips one last time, Lacht made a decision and almost fell over a fallen log as she turned toward the stream. Quickly, she knelt beside the stream and cupped her hands under the flowing current. When she lifted her hands toward her mouth, golden liquid came up inside them, so she put her mouth next to it, tilted her head back, and made sipping and swallowing movements. Had anything gone down her throat?

She didn't have time for this. She had to hurry!

Closing her eyes, Lacht lowered her head until it went under the water. When she opened her eyes once more, a dot of a fish whisked past her. It was a red polka dot of a fish, and she smiled at its tiny impertinence.

Then she made swallowing movements with her throat again.

I must look like a fish; a big fish with long black hair, she thought and gulped away.

Two minutes of gulping satisfied her thirst, and she sprang up, automatically raising both hands to push back wet hair, but only soft dry strands touched her fingers.

"Of course," she muttered. "Wet Ones stay dry! Irsht was

84

right. They should have called us *Dry Ones*."

"Hurry up," insisted the stream.

Lacht hurried, but thirty minutes later, she wondered if she'd made a mistake. Surely, she should have reached the pond by now.

The trees continued on either side of the stream as far as she could see—tall, dark gold trunks blending into more tall, dark gold trunks. The dark gold of the tree trunks and the lighter gold of the stream contrasted beautifully, making an attractive picture—with the forest's blue leaves forming an overhead canopy. But she had thought that thought too many times over the past few minutes and didn't want to think it again. Walking down a short slope, she kept her eyes half-closed so she wouldn't see anything, attractive or otherwise.

Consequently, she walked knee deep into the pond before realizing where she was. With a gasp, she leapt backwards to dry land. Then she stared across the surface of the water, heart pounding.

On the other side of the pond, trees grew thickly to the water's edge. Wisps of mists were beginning to break out of the pond, indicating the end of the midday hours. The dark gold tree trunks standing behind the light gold, misty water created an attractive picture, especially with the blue leaves on the tree branches overhead providing contrast.

Did I think that again? Did I really think it again?

Glaring at the scene before her, the young Stalli woman stood rigidly in place and wished she could go home.

It was one thing to announce to Ploddin her intent to join the Wassandra girl. It was another thing altogether to stand on the edge of the pond, the real pond, trying to work up the courage to stay there, much less walk into the water.

Lacht wanted desperately to soar up into the air as she had in her dream—far, far up into the air and away from this horrible pond. She glanced at the woods on her left and then swung her gaze rapidly to the right.

"There are too many trees in these mountains!" she muttered

crossly, then stared down—anywhere but straight ahead.

A few minutes passed while she studied her feet, which stood as if rooted in the short, grassy bank that bordered the water on this side of the pond. A bug climbed up a blue blade of grass and sunbathed. She watched it enviously.

Abruptly, the bug flew away, and, just as abruptly, she sat on the grass and tried to draw a deep, calming breath. The result sounded like a prolonged whimper, and she had started on another one, when a soft tongue came out of nowhere and licked her ear.

She knew that tongue.

"Brownie," she whispered shakily, "I guess you do follow me."

The little dog squirmed with pleasure, and Lacht whispered and crooned over him, trying to forget why she'd come. But the small body of the dog reminded her of the Wassandra girl all curled up on the floor of her cave, so thin and helpless.

Brownie reached up and licked Lacht's ear again. A rush of emotion filled her; she could not let that poor girl down. She swallowed hard and made herself study the golden pond.

The early afternoon mists didn't hide the wide circle of thicker gold on the right side of the pond, the circle that had curving bits of branches rising above the water in places. She'd seen it in her dream the night before, but she hadn't known what it was then. Now she knew.

It's the top of the panotka plant!

She shuddered and half-closed her eyes, but immediately another picture of the trapped girl flitted into her mind. The girl huddled on the floor of the cave this time, with her arms around her knees. She was crying.

Lacht stood as abruptly as she had sat and walked to the edge of the pond.

Hey! Over there, wasn't that the very cone-shaped rock she'd clung to in her dream? Yes, it was, and next to it grew the water-reeds she'd grabbed in a futile effort to stop her descent into the water. She walked closer and stared curiously at the reeds. Had she pulled any of them out?

Can you do that in a dream? Whoa! Stop it, Lacht! You're delaying again.

When she stepped into the water between the cone-shaped rock and the water reeds, Brownie whined from the shore.

"Go home, Brownie," she ordered, turning around and shooing with one hand. "Go home to Ploddin."

She turned back around, took a deep breath—and held it. Her body refused to budge. Lacht made her lungs take another breath, but she couldn't make her body take another step.

"Keshua," she whispered and saying his name reminded her of his love.

"Keshua," she whispered again, forcing one foot a few inches forward and dragging the other one after it.

As the golden water closed over her head, she heard Brownie barking from the shore of the pond.

Ploddin slammed the head of his hammer down on the bench and glared at it. Over an hour had passed, and he hadn't been able to do anything right, not since Lacht had left.

After all the effort he had put into building up his fire that morning, he'd let it cool off toward the end of their talk. When Lacht had run away, he'd pumped anger as well as air through the old bellows and broken them; and now, when he'd finally managed to get a hot fire going again, he'd hammered the latch of a gate in when it needed to go out.

"Hello," Winnel said, walking up to the yard and leaning on the fence. "Have you seen Lacht?"

The young man scowled at the name. "She was here," he growled.

"Did she say where she meant to go next?" her father asked.

Ploddin hesitated. "No," he finally said.

"Well, if you see her, let her know I'm looking for her,"

Winnel responded gently and walked off.

The blacksmith stared at the hammer in front of him. He hadn't lied. He didn't know where Lacht had gone. He only knew she'd left at an angry run.

Brownie was gone too. Ploddin had wasted a good ten minutes peering under his porch to see if the little dog lay in its dark recesses. Irrationally, he had thought that if Brownie cringed somewhere in the shadows, Lacht would come back—she'd come back to see the dog. But Brownie was gone.

Making himself pick up a long iron rod, he put one of its ends into the forge and heated it. When the metal glowed red, he pulled it out and hammered it into a sharp point that would go into the ground and hold a gate firmly in place.

Use iron to fight a Wert but make sure it has not rusted. Werts do not object to rusted metal, but they cannot abide the touch of clean iron.

"Keshua, deliver me from a fired-up memory," Ploddin groaned out loud, seeing in his mind the information page next to the picture of the Wert as clearly as if he had read the child's book yesterday instead of years and years ago.

"Get back to work," he groused at himself and picked up the iron piece to inspect it for smoothness.

He liked his gates perfectly smooth so that anyone passing by could run a hand down the iron lengths without danger of being nicked by a sharp spot.

"It's smooth," he muttered with a nod, but when he found himself searching for rust, he threw the rod down in disgust and stomped inside to make an early lunch.

Crispin arrived home a few minutes later and made his own lunch. The two brothers munched at the kitchen table in silence, but Ploddin eventually cocked his head in his older brother's direction. Crispin didn't usually stay silent this long.

"Something wrong?" he finally asked.

"The wise ones rebuked us," Crispin complained and threw the remains of his third sandwich on the table. "They say we've told lies about the Wassandra, spreading fear with our stories, and making it difficult for Wassandra and Stallis to live as neighbors."

"Well, I have heard talk," commented Ploddin dryly.

Crispin's arms spread wide to indicate his innocence. Ploddin had seen that gesture hundreds of times, but he stopped chewing when the edges of his brother's mouth curved downward. Crispin never frowned.

"We didn't mean any harm. It was only lighthearted fun. Nobody should have taken us seriously."

Ploddin stared, fire beginning to smolder in his dark brown eyes. All those years of hiding; all those years of hearing crude stories about Wet Ones; all those years—

"Let's hope the Wassandra didn't do the same thing," he said sharply.

"What?" questioned Crispin, as if he had never considered such a thing. "What do you mean?"

"Stallis, ugh! Don't go near them. You know what they're like—abnormally short-limbed creatures with stubs on the ends of their hands instead of fingers, dark mold hanging in strips from their heads, and mud balls for eyes," suggested Ploddin. "Do you think the Wassandra described us in that way to their children—in their lighthearted moments, of course, and all in fun?"

Crispin looked askance at Ploddin. The younger brother didn't often criticize the older. Ploddin had grown sullen and sour over the years, but Crispin had always thought his little brother's moodiness resulted from working too hard.

"Imaginations have to be controlled as much and as often as anything else," growled Ploddin in his best sourplum manner.

"You should get out more; make friends," Crispin growled back.

"You're probably right," snapped Ploddin, much to his brother's surprise.

"Well then, you're right too," Crispin agreed, suddenly cheerful again. "I'll try to control my imagination."

He smiled at Ploddin, and the fire in the younger man's eyes died away.

"I tell you what. I'll finish the bedposts today," offered Crispin with a magnanimous hand flourish.

His brother's face swiveled up towards the ceiling. "*You* are volunteering to work?" he asked in an unnaturally high squeak. "*You?*"

"I've done it before," Crispin defended himself, "once or twice."

The two brothers smiled at each other, their harmony restored. They finished lunch a little after noon, and Ploddin went outside in a better mood to work on his gate. Picking up another piece of iron, he inspected it for rough places and found several he'd need to smooth out.

But no rust, he caught himself musing before sticking it into the fire.

He worked steadily for two hours, only lifting his head at the sound of feet pounding toward him.

Irsht started shouting before she rounded the corner. "Ploddin, we can't find Lacht. She left home this morning for the first time in days, but she didn't come back for lunch and we're worried. Have you seen her?"

"Not since this morning," he answered slowly.

Irsht ran off toward town, and he frowned.

You don't suppose—

Filling a bucket with coal, he carried it to his forge. Lacht didn't know where to find the Wassandra girl. She couldn't possibly know. Nobody knew. It would take directions from Keshua himself to—

Ploddin dumped the shiny black nuggets next to the fire instead of into it and stared at them without noticing what he'd done. *That's impossible! Keshua did not give Lacht dreams!*

Someone else started running toward him on the road then, a little someone this time, whose feet pattered, instead of pounding, even at a run. When he jerked his head up to identify the new arrival, his jaw dropped.

Brownie stood in the middle of the road, where the sun could shine directly on him. That was surprising enough, considering the dog's shyness; but Brownie wasn't just standing there waiting for someone to spot him.

He was barking, loudly and continuously, head thrust forward and tail stuck out behind him. The little dog's body stiffened with purpose, as he put every ounce of energy he possessed into barking at Ploddin.

Ten

Under the Pond

A fter her head went under the surface of the pond, Lacht couldn't keep her balance. She'd negotiated the steep slope in her dream, but this wasn't a dream anymore. One more step and she fell, tumbling in somersaults down an uncompromising incline.

Fortunately, the golden water lessened the impact of her fall. It didn't buoy her upwards like normal water, but she could feel it all around her, making the tumbling less jarring. With a final somersault, she slid into a pile of fallen leaves at the bottom of the pond.

The Wert!

She pushed her head out of the purple leaves, her heart racing. No orange body with snake-like arms and lidless eyes squatted on the pond floor, and she sagged with relief, but only for a few seconds. The cavern of darkness she had seen in her dream lurked all too ominously on her left.

The Wert had come from there.

Jumping up, she ran toward the long, waving panotka leaves on her right. As she neared them, her concern grew. The outside layer of leaves had already fallen and drifted into piles like the one she had just slid into; the leaves still hanging had thinned until she could see through them. At least they still provided shelter.

Burrowing into the panotka plant, like a Root child burrowing into a cave, Lacht found herself entering a fragile purple world. As she neared the middle of the plant, where the leaves hung closer together, her heart began to slow down.

Finally, she pushed into the small enclosure at the panotka's center and let the last leaves fall behind her.

"Hi!" said a voice.

Lacht stared at the Wassandra girl, sitting all huddled up, reed-thin arms around her knees. Without a word, Lacht knelt on the floor of the cave and held out her arms.

"I knew you'd come," said the girl as she went into Lacht's embrace and hugged her.

"How did you?" asked Lacht, fighting back tears.

It was right to be there, so very right that, despite the danger, her strongest emotion was gratitude. She'd done it. With the Plete's help, she'd done it, and now the Wassandra girl wasn't alone anymore.

"Keshua told me you'd come," answered the girl, drawing back to see her face, "but he didn't tell me your name. What's your name?"

Lacht smiled at the girl—curious, despite everything that had happened to her. "My name is Lacht. What's your name?"

"Curl," moaned that individual with a prolonged sigh evidently aimed toward her name.

It was obvious where the name had come from, even in the dim light of the cave, because the eleven-year-old's hair curled in short ringlets around her head. Curl sighed again with depressed resignation.

"Curl is a beautiful name," Lacht offered.

"It's the commonest of all common names," the Wassandra girl corrected her, "except for Wave or Mist. I tried to get my parents to change it to Lacy Froth, but—Wassandra do not have two names, just one, and you have to keep the one we gave you!" With those last words, she changed her tone to one of reprimand.

Lacht laughed appreciatively.

"Have you come to take me out?" asked Curl next.

The young woman nodded hesitantly. She hadn't let herself

plan that far ahead, and her dreams had not given her any instructions. "I will certainly try," she answered with as much courage as she could muster.

Then her mustered courage disappeared, sinking, as far as she could tell, into the ground beneath her feet.

"The Wert's coming," whimpered Curl and hid her face in Lacht's shirt.

"It can't get in," she said in an overloud voice. "The panotka leaves will keep it away."

"They're falling," came the girl's muffled reply. "They fall more and more every day."

"It'll go away," Lacht insisted, "and then we'll sneak out in the opposite direction."

"Do you think I haven't tried that?" Curl asked indignantly, her head tilting sideways to give her words more volume. "It knows when I move through the leaves. It's always there in front of me; or else it's coming so fast that I don't have time. Even if I could cross the bottom of the pond, I'd have to climb the slope, and that slope's steep!"

"Yes, I know," Lacht agreed, lowering her head to rest on Curl's.

How would they get out? *Would* they get out? Fear didn't stab this time—it suffocated. Lacht could hardly breathe, as if the thick fear had clogged up her nose. She sneezed it out and hugged Curl.

"Listen, Curl," she whispered, "Keshua brought me here for a reason. I don't know what he'll do next, but he wouldn't have sent me all those dreams if he hadn't meant to rescue you."

Closing her eyes, Lacht hoped she'd told the truth. At least, her words had the effect of distracting Curl.

The Wassandra girl didn't tilt her head away again from Lacht's shirt, which she evidently meant to absorb into her face, but she did ask with renewed curiosity, "What dreams?"

Lacht described her dreams, one at a time, making each description last as long as possible, so they could think about

94

something besides the Wert.

"Did you pull out any water reeds in your last dream?" asked Curl.

"I wondered about that too," she said. "I started to check on my way into the water, but Keshua wouldn't let me. I guess he wanted me to hurry down here and keep you company."

A thin face separated from her shirt and peered up at her. "I'm glad you came," Curl stated impulsively, "I love you, Lacht."

"I love you too, Curl," Lacht responded, smiling slightly.

She hadn't known her long, but Lacht suspected that impulsive statements came quite naturally to the younger girl, who probably expressed anger as easily as love. Either way, no one would have to wonder what Curl was feeling.

Lacht's throat tightened.

Precious girl! Precious Wassandra girl! No wonder her people felt frantic enough to contact us.

They quit talking then. The Wert must have moved away, because they could breathe normally again. Curl sighed heavily, and her head drooped against the comforting shirt. Lacht sat very still and let her sleep.

She couldn't see the girl clearly, except for her short curls and thin arms. The subdued light in the cave didn't illuminate the walls of panotka leaves very well either, but she knew they were purple, far too purple.

Staring at the leaves in front of her, she singled one out and watched it swirl upward until it disappeared in the dim apex of the cave. As she looked up, the long leaf broke loose and fell in graceful spirals to the cave floor.

Lacht didn't single out any other leaves. She sat, holding Curl, and the muscles in her back got sore before the younger girl finally moved, then yawned.

"Did I fall 'sleep?" she asked drowsily.

"Yes," Lacht told her, smiling at the sleep-drenched face. "You must have needed a nap."

"I sleep more and more," Curl complained, "and I'm sick of

pooma."

"What's pooma?" asked Lacht.

"You don't know what pooma is?" responded Curl, sitting upright and staring at Lacht. "I wish I didn't! Pooma is leaves and roots mixed together into a stick. Pooma lasts forever, which is why I got some for my trip. I liked it at first. Mama knows how to sweeten it."

Her face twisted. "I miss her," she whispered. "I'm sorry I ran away."

"I know you are," Lacht told her. "She'll forgive you."

They sat a few minutes longer.

"Do you want some?" finally asked Curl.

"Some pooma?" questioned Lacht.

The Wassandra girl nodded and moved behind her. She rummaged in a backpack and brought out four thick, stubby sticks that did not, to tell the truth, look extremely appetizing.

"Pooma!" she announced triumphantly. "I've only got four left."

"Uh, I've already eaten today," Lacht answered, staring at the meager food supply and wishing she'd thought to bring something. "You go ahead."

"Okay," she agreed, popping the end of a stick into her mouth, "but I'd rather have a boogleberry shake. They are *so* good! What would you rather have?"

"A cinnamon roll," answered Lacht immediately, remembering the special treats she had enjoyed so recently, "or a piece of blueberry pie."

"When we get out of here," Curl stated rather thickly around her mouthful of pooma, "I want to try those things."

"Okay," agreed Lacht, "and I want to try a boogleberry shake. What's in it?"

"Boogleberries mixed with lake froth," Curl said, moving the stick to the side of her mouth so she could bite a piece off. "I don't know what else, but it all grows in the lake. Mama makes great boogleberry shakes," she added, but the mention of her mother made the girl's face twist again.

"How did Keshua let you know I was coming?" asked Lacht hastily in an effort to distract her.

"He told me," she answered matter-of-factly, "two days ago. He gave me a hug and said you'd get here soon."

"You mean Keshua came here, to this cave?" Lacht asked loudly, her eyes doubling in size as she forgot about distracting Curl.

Curl nodded as she chewed busily.

"Keshua has never come to me," Lacht told the girl in front of her enviously, "not where I could see him. You are so lucky!"

Then she stared around at the dark water and the pooma sticks and the thin leaves—and couldn't hold back a smile. What had she just said?

Curl began to laugh and almost choked before she swallowed down her bite of pooma. "Oh, bursting bubbles, I am so lucky," she chortled at last. "What nice pooma I have!"

"And such long leaves," pointed out Lacht.

"And a dark cave," added Curl, giggling.

They laughed companionably for as long as they could make it last.

"Well," Lacht said, when she couldn't laugh anymore. "Really, it is special to have Keshua come to you. He came to Lynn too, you know."

"Who's Lynn?" asked Curl.

The Wassandra girl had finished her pooma stick and seemed to be getting a drink of water. Her mouth opened and closed, while her throat made swallowing movements. She did it quite naturally. Lacht watched and promised herself that she would drink only when Curl couldn't see her.

Curl looks like a normal person getting a drink of water, not a fish with a gulping mouth.

"Lynn was a young woman about my age. Keshua brought her to Tarth from another world," she began.

Curl leaned against her shoulder during the story, which

Lacht told in great detail. When she'd finished, the Wassandra commented, "That's a good story. Do you think it really happened?"

"Yes, I know Lynn and Chell. We lived in the desert with the Stalli volunteers and met Lynn when she first came to Tarth."

"Is she still alive?" Curl asked next.

When she nodded, the girl announced, "I want to meet her!"

"You can meet Lynn and her family this fall," Lacht agreed. "They're supposed to visit us then," but the corners of her mouth curved down as she said the words.

Would they ever get out?

I don't think so.

Curl moved next to her and pushed her face against Lacht's dress. "It's coming," she whimpered.

They sat and fought their feelings of panic, but the fears grew steadily worse—not suffocating, but stabbing like sharp knives again. They cut into Lacht's mind deeper and deeper. She didn't think she could move. What had Ploddin said? Something about the Wert paralyzing its victims?

She wasn't paralyzed yet! With an effort, she stood up, pulling Curl with her. "The Wert's coming through the leaves," she said shrilly. "We've got to get out of here. It'll hypnotize us if we see its eyes."

Curl shook visibly, even in the dim light of the cave, but she put a finger on her lips and tugged at Lacht's arm.

Fear didn't make Lacht shake; it made her want to repeat everything she had said, only louder this time. She closed her mouth and made it stay closed as she followed the Wassandra girl. Curl didn't need to hear about the Wert. She'd grown up in Wasso Lake. She knew all about underwater monsters.

They hurried through the leaves, retracing Lacht's steps, because the fear knives were coming from the opposite direction. Maybe the Wert had gone around the plant until it found a thinned-out section of leaves.

Lacht hoped desperately that the leaves on their side would

stop it, but as they reached the last layers, every leaf they brushed past pulled loose from its high mooring. The panotka plant had died that afternoon. It could no longer protect them.

Even so, both girls winced when they stepped out of the leaves onto the empty floor of the pond, but they had no time to waste regretting the loss of their shelter. Side by side, they ran across the floor of the pond toward the steep slope Lacht had slid down three hours ago.

You can't run fast in water, not even golden water, Lacht's mind chattered fearfully. *Curl doesn't know how to go any faster than I do.*

One of her legs made a slow bound forward, then the other leg took its measured turn; however, they'd almost crossed the flat part. In one or two more bounds, they could—

Without warning, the Wert landed ten feet away on their right side. Someone screamed loudly, and she never knew whether the scream had come out of her or Curl. The two girls shrank away from the squat, orange body, shielding their faces from its eyes.

The Wert bent its right knee and jumped to their left, long arms undulating out on either side. As soon as it landed, it bent its left knee and jumped back to their right.

"It's playing with us," Curl said shakily.

The monster's mouth opened, and, beneath her sheltering hands, Lacht could see an orange tongue writhing forward over two rows of teeth.

"Keshua!" she shouted with all the strength left in her.

"Keshua!" Curl shouted in a responsive echo.

The Wert bent both knees as it prepared to move again, this time straight at them.

With a thump, a body landed on the floor of the pond between the two girls and the monster.

"Lacht, get her out of here," snapped a familiar voice.

"Ploddin!" gasped Lacht.

The Wert had backed up a step or two. It didn't like whatever Ploddin was waving in its face. Nevertheless, it didn't want to leave, not with fresh meat so tantalizingly close. One of its arms made a sudden grab at Ploddin.

He banged the arm with a long black stick of some kind, and the Wert howled in pain. Its mouth opened into a circle when it howled, a teeth-rimmed circle. Lacht watched under her hand shield. She couldn't look away.

Curl was pulling at her arm, though, and she allowed the younger girl to pull her backwards, one step at a time.

Ploddin.

"Go on!" ordered Ploddin, as if he could see her hesitation, though his eyes never left the Wert's knees.

He must have seen the monster's knees bend before it moved to either side of the girls. He must have come down the steep slope just in time to learn that revealing fact. Then he had jumped in between them.

Lacht took another step back, her face turned toward Ploddin and the Wert. Shouldn't she help?

The Wert lunged to the left and reached at Ploddin from several different directions. Two of its long arms almost touched him, fingernails clacking together in anticipation, but he sprang up in the water and stuck the point of his stick into one of the arms as it snaked beneath him.

The ensuing howl bounced off their side of the pond and clamored its way to the other. Both girls flinched, and Curl let go of Lacht to cover her ears.

The point of the stick had stuck in the Wert's arm. Ploddin tugged at it, but it didn't come out right away. The other arms whipped toward him, and the Wert stopped howling and cackled at its opportunity.

Right before the attacking arms reached him, Ploddin whacked one of them with the other end of the stick, and the sideways motion pulled the point clear.

"Lacht, Keshua sent you to rescue that girl. Now get busy and do it!" he shouted, and his familiar crossness freed Lacht from inaction.

"Let's go, Curl," she said, reaching for the younger girl's hand; and the two of them bounded through the water once more, but this time they bounded up the steep, underwater slope.

We're going to fall, panicked Lacht, *we're going to fall and slide back down*; but Curl knew how to run up steep slopes. Holding her body at an angle, the Wassandra girl landed on her toes, throwing her free hand out for balance, and Lacht copied her.

The long weeks of imprisonment had weakened Curl, though. Halfway up the slope, she slowed down, gasping for breath. Lacht had to grab the younger girl around the waist, then propel both of them forward at the necessary angle. Somehow, they kept going.

Another step, just one more; now another, please another.

With a brilliance that hurt their eyes, the sun shot its shafts at them as their heads broke above the surface of the pond. The girls staggered through the shallows and out of the water. They didn't stop until they'd gone two feet up the short bank. Then Lacht collapsed onto the grass, and Curl bumped down next to her.

"We're out. We're out. We made it!" sang Curl with a radiant smile, peeking between her fingers at the sun and the trees and the grass, and blinking hard to accustom her eyes to sunlight after all the weeks of semidarkness.

Lacht didn't respond. She didn't even hear the happy girl. Pushing herself into a sitting position and blinking as her eyes adjusted more quickly than Curl's, she stared at the pond.

It lay still and serene under the late afternoon mists that swirled above its surface. The mists would lift higher and higher as evening came, until Tarth's nightlights danced in the night sky. Then the mists would dance too, three feet above their golden home.

Tears trickled down her cheeks.

She started when Curl put an arm around her neck. The younger girl had adjusted somewhat to the light, enough to take her fingers away from her eyes. She clutched a fistful of sun-warmed grass with one hand, but her other tried to wipe Lacht's wet cheeks.

"Who's down there?" she asked.

"Ploddin, a friend of mine," Lacht whispered. "I don't know how he—"

"Look," Curl interrupted abruptly, pointing at a nearby bush.

Lacht obediently turned her head, though she couldn't see anything at first. Then she spotted the small brown head.

"Brownie, you brought Ploddin, didn't you?" she asked in a broken voice, holding a hand out toward the little dog.

Hesitatingly, with an eye on the newcomer, Brownie slid out of the bush.

Curl knew no hesitation. "Brownie," she shouted, "you're the most wonderful animal I've ever seen!"

Fortunately, Curl's weakened state did not allow her shout to reach intimidation level. Brownie's ears cringed back and his tail went down, but he crept closer.

"You've never seen a dog before?" asked Lacht absentmindedly.

"No, is that what he is?" the Wassandra girl questioned back with delight. "It's not fair that you Stallis have better animals than we do!"

Brownie reached them then, and as Curl stroked the soft hairs on his head and back, the little dog lost all his normal reserve. He crawled into Lacht's lap and licked both of their faces.

Curl shrieked with delight, and Brownie whined in ecstasy. Only Lacht stayed silent, staring at the golden surface of the pond.

When the water started moving, she sprang to her feet, knocking Curl away and dumping Brownie onto the ground. Neither girl nor dog cared. They were staring at the water now too.

Ripples were erupting from deep within the pond, ripples that made tiny waves slosh against the bank. Then a dark spot appeared and spread out in a widening circle, visible even through the mists.

"What's happening?" asked Curl, but Lacht had wanted to ask her the same question.

She shook her head helplessly and her eyes widened

unnaturally. When Brownie leaned trembling against Curl, the girl put an arm around the little dog. In her peripheral vision, Lacht could see the two of them sitting on the grass next to her, but she didn't turn toward them.

The dark stain trumped its way over the golden water.

Lacht stood with a hand at her throat, until the stain reached the edge of the bank. Then she screamed, "Ploddin!" and took a quick step toward the pond.

"Don't touch that water," gasped Curl.

Lacht stopped short, but not because of Curl.

Eleven

Ploddin

"What kind of a welcome do you call that!" someone protested.

On Lacht's left, where the stream from Wasso Lake still poured golden water into the stained pond, a head poked up above the tall water reeds—Ploddin's head.

Lacht stared at him, her mouth falling open. How had he gotten there?

"Up until now, only my leg limped. Now I think my ears might well—"

"Ears don't limp!" Lacht shouted into the young man's complaint.

She ran into the stream and knelt beside him, hugging him close. He hugged her back for a long minute.

"You know," he then remarked conversationally, "Wet Ones do have advantages, after all. For example, I can sit in this golden stream without getting wet. On the other hand, your tears have drenched the front of my shirt. Do you think we could get up? I want to meet the Wassandra girl who caused all this trouble."

"It wasn't me. I didn't cause the trouble," immediately stated a voice from over beside Brownie. "The Wert did."

"Oh yes, the Wert did it all, did he?" Ploddin responded as he limped over the blue grass toward her.

"Well, I kind of ran away," admitted Curl, "but I wished I hadn't. I wished I hadn't lots of times."

"I bet you did," he agreed, kneeling beside her and laying a hand on Brownie's head. "Brownie led me to you," he said over his shoulder.

"I figured that much out," replied Lacht as she slowly approached the other two. She felt a little shaky still. "Ploddin, the Wert—?"

"It's dead," he told her. "I killed it with an iron rod that was supposed to hold up a gate. That rod made a good weapon. It made a good walking stick too, point up, though it was heavy out of the water, and Brownie insisted on coming straight here—I mean, literally straight here. He chose the shortest possible route, no doubt; but a dog can run faster than a person, even a person without a limp, and underbrush didn't slow Brownie down. He wiggled through in seconds, then barked until I caught up."

"How did you kill the Wert?" Curl asked, brightening with curiosity. "Didn't it try to paralyze you?"

"It tried," the young man responded as he sat on the grass and leaned back on his elbows, stretching his legs out in front of him with a sigh of relief. "However, I'd read the book, and I knew better than to look at its eyes."

"I never read the book," Lacht felt compelled to say. "You told me about the Wert's eyes, but I never saw the explanation in print."

"Yes, I believe you now," he said, squinting at her apologetically. "I'm sorry I didn't believe you before."

"The Wert," Curl reminded him, bouncing up and down on the grass. "I want to hear about the Wert."

"Nasty, ugly, orange thing," he commented, lying all the way back on the warm blue grass and putting his hands behind his head. "Why on Tarth would you want to hear about it? You should've had enough of that monster to last a lifetime."

"He's interesting now that we're safe out here," Curl insisted. "How did you kill him?"

"Werts don't like iron," he explained lazily, his eyes half-closing, as if he were about to fall asleep, but Lacht knew better.

He was teasing the Wassandra girl, and she refused to allow it. Curl may have run away from home, but she had certainly suffered for it. If she wanted to know about that monster, then—

"Ploddin, tell Curl about the Wert," she ordered.

"Curl, is it!" Ploddin drawled, opening his eyes. "All right, Curl, I'll tell you, but only once, and I will not answer detailed questions. It's not my favorite topic of conversation."

He sat up and gazed at the water. Lacht glanced at it along with him and shuddered slightly.

Already, the current in the fast moving stream had pushed the stain back a few feet. Gold would triumph eventually, making the pond beautiful once more; but she never wanted to see that part of the Stalli Mountains again, beautiful or not!

Turning toward Ploddin again, she was just in time to see the muscles in his face tighten. His expression didn't resemble a sourplum yet, but it was in the first stages. When his whole body went tense, responsive tears pushed at the back of her eyes.

If Ploddin hadn't arrived when he did....

"The Wert put up a good fight," he began, breaking into her thoughts.

"It almost got me a couple of times, with all those arms. I felt like I was fighting several monsters at once. Fortunately, it really did hate iron. All I had to do was touch my rod to one of its arms, and it would pull all of them back, howling in pain. Finally, I got close enough to stick the point of the rod into its body.

"I knew I must have killed it when it didn't howl. Its mouth opened, but no sound came out, only an oily ooze. At first, the ooze trickled, then it gushed, and the water got dark all around the Wert. The darkness began spreading, so I ran for it.

"You know, I'm not as lame underwater as I am on land. I ran remarkably well, only the fighting had turned me in circles, and I didn't know where to come up—not that I felt particularly picky. Anywhere out of that ooze suited me. When the current of the stream pushed against me, I followed it out.

"I was lying in the streambed, catching my breath, when the

highest pitched scream ever uttered on Tarth burst into the air. I thought my ears—"

"All right, Ploddin, that's enough," Lacht told him, smiling.

Curl was smiling too. "Stallis have black hair," she remarked with great interest. "Your hair looked dark gold in the cave, Lacht."

"I know," she agreed. "So did yours."

Lacht gazed with appreciation at the Wassandra. Curl's skin gleamed pale gold under golden clothing of a slightly darker hue. Her long arms were graceful, rather than grotesque; and her long fingers waved with supple movements in the air whenever she talked.

"You talk with your fingers as much as your mouth," Lacht marveled.

"You have the prettiest, dark brown eyes," responded Curl. "All Wassandra have golden eyes. Everything is golden in Wasso Lake. It's so boring!"

She laughed at the gold-hating girl and looked admiringly at Curl's eyes, flecked by light brown bits of color. "Your hair's brown," she pointed out.

"Yes, but it has golden highlights," Curl complained.

Ploddin's body had relaxed now that he'd quit talking about the Wert. Lacht wanted to stretch out next to him on the warm blue grass and take a nap, but she gave a great sigh instead.

"We need to return Curl to her parents," she said reluctantly.

Ploddin nodded and pushed himself onto his feet with a groan.

"You're right," he agreed.

Withering, Curl buried her head in Brownie's soft side.

"They'll yell at me," she whimpered.

"Not at first," the young Stalli man corrected her cheerfully. "That'll happen later. Come on."

He reached out his arms, and, without any further objection, the girl catapulted into them.

"Hey, don't you think you can walk?" asked Lacht.

Curl was weak and thin, but surely she could walk a little ways.

"No," replied Curl contentedly.

"Well! I think you could walk some!" Lacht insisted, wondering how she could offer to carry the girl instead of Ploddin without hurting his feelings.

"I like Wet Ones," was Curl's only answer, as she lay her head down on Ploddin's shoulder.

He moved off, following the stream, and Brownie scampered behind, tail wagging. Lacht followed the three of them, watching carefully and wincing whenever Ploddin's limp got worse. At least, all that blacksmithing had strengthened his arms. As the minutes passed, he held Curl without any sign of strain, and she began to relax.

Why worry? It takes too much energy.

A big yawn pushed itself out of her body, and then a series of smaller yawns followed, one after another.

Tired.

When her stomach gave a loud rumble, Lacht rubbed it apologetically. She felt hungry enough to eat pooma, but they'd left the pooma sticks under the pond, and she didn't want to think about that pond anymore.

Her mind shifted, and she asked, "Curl, do you know how we got the name, Wet Ones? I mean, we don't get wet in Wasso Lake. We stay dry. Why did they name us *Wet Ones?*"

Curl peered sleepily over Ploddin's shoulder and yawned before she answered Lacht. "The Wassandra named you that a long time ago. Don't you feel the smooth wetness whenever you come into the water, like something soft all over you?"

"That's not what wet feels like," Lacht said. "Wet means having water drip on you, and your hair gets soggy, and your clothes feel damp, and your shoes and socks go ooshy gooshy."

She found it hard to describe wetness to someone who had obviously never experienced such a thing.

"No, that's not wet," argued Curl, perking up. "Wet is like

having a cushion all around you wherever you are—a nice soft cushion. Wasso Lake isn't that bad really, I suppose. Do you like it, Ploddin?"

"I don't know," he told her. "I've never been in it."

"Oh, I can't wait to show you two around," Curl said enthusiastically.

The Wassandra girl showed no vestiges of droopiness now. In fact, she bounced up and down so hard that Ploddin had to tell her to stop.

"But how did people from Stalli ever become Wet Ones to begin with?" Lacht asked, glad to be getting answers finally to her questions.

"A Wassandra married a Stalli long ago," Curl explained. "Their children were Wet Ones."

"That makes sense. Their descendents over the years must have varied," Ploddin said thoughtfully. "Some of them became Wet Ones, and others didn't."

"What would happen if a Wet One married a Wassandra?" Lacht wondered out loud.

"Let's do it!" Curl shouted. "I'll marry a Wet One, and we'll see what happens." The eleven-year-old shook her head regretfully at Ploddin. "I'd marry you, but it's obvious you're taken. Do you have a brother?"

Ploddin snorted loud enough to frighten a small flock of birds out of the tree in front of them, and Lacht burst into laughter.

"What are you laughing at?" Curl asked. The light brown flecks in the younger girl's eyes started hopping sideways, giving a mischievous glint to the golden eyes that peered at her over Ploddin's shoulder. "Don't you know what I meant when I said Ploddin was taken? I meant—"

"I'm laughing," Lacht hastily interrupted her, "because Ploddin's brother, Crispin, is too old for you, and he's not a Wet One. Besides, Crispin made up stories about the Wassandra, scary stories. He'll be surprised to discover what a beautiful people you are."

The young Wassandra wrinkled her nose. "We tell stupid stories about you too," she admitted. "Crispin won't be the only one surprised."

"A lot of good might come out of this," began Ploddin.

Curl lost the wrinkles around her nose. "That's right," she said enthusiastically. "We can tell that to my parents."

Stumbling as he stepped over a big tree trunk, Ploddin had to take a quick step to one side before he could regain his balance.

"It doesn't make what you did right," he reminded Curl a little breathlessly.

Lacht hopped over the tree trunk after him and asked before her feet hit the ground, "Curl, don't you want me to take you for a while?"

"No," the girl answered with conviction. She put her arms around Ploddin's neck. "Ploddin's stronger than you are—and a lot handsomer," she finished with another mischievous peek.

Ploddin snorted again, and Lacht smiled; then her face brightened even further. Their conversation had taken attention away from the actual walking. Ahead of them, through the trees, golden water poured over the surface of a big, gray rock.

When he reached the waterfall, Ploddin put Curl on her feet. Blowing a little, he sat on a small rock next to the stream. Then he turned pink.

Lacht started slightly as she sat near him. *Is it sunset already?*

Ploddin, evidently, was thinking the opposite. "How could so much happen in such a short time?" he asked, shaking his head.

Curl glanced at the beautiful pink about her, but the exploring girl had seen sunsets before, and she had other things on her mind. "You'll come home with me, won't you?" she begged the two of them. "My parents won't get as angry if you're there."

"Curl, is that all you can think about?" Lacht asked severely. "Don't you care that your parents have worried about you for weeks?"

The Wassandra hung her head, but Ploddin spoke before she could. "I'll take her from here, Lacht. You should return to Burkin

Village. Your family's been worried about you too this afternoon."

"That means telling them I'm a Wet One all by myself," she protested, jumping up from her rock and wringing her hands. "I don't want to do that."

"You can wait until I get back to the village to tell about us," Ploddin pointed out. "Your family—"

"But I want to take Curl home too," she interrupted.

"Lacht, don't you care that your parents have worried about you for hours today?" Curl scolded promptly. "Shame, shame, shame on you!"

Ploddin laughed, and even Lacht couldn't keep a smile off her face though she tried. Smirking, the eleven-year-old proceeded to organize everything.

"Lacht doesn't have to walk around Wasso Lake," she announced. "Going through is shorter. I can show her the way before Ploddin and I go home."

"How much longer would it take?" her escort asked suspiciously, "and are you sure which direction to go once we're under the water?" he added. "It's a big lake."

"I know Wasso Lake well enough that I got bored with it," wheedled Curl. "That's why I left. It won't take long."

Ploddin thought a minute, then nodded at Lacht. "It ought to shorten your trip," he admitted. "Why don't you come with us?"

Lacht smiled broadly. She wouldn't have to part from them right away. She could go down into the golden water with them.

"OH NO!" screamed Curl.

Ploddin jumped to his feet, and Lacht's body tensed convulsively.

"I'll have to say good-bye to Brownie!" the Wassandra girl wailed. "Dogs can't breathe under Wasso Lake."

Ploddin groaned loudly, and Lacht would have echoed him if she'd had the energy.

"Don't scare us like that, Curl," she said, holding onto a tree trunk for support. "We've had enough scares for one day."

Curl threw herself on the ground beside Brownie and gave

the little dog a hug. "I'll visit you," she promised.

Brownie licked Curl's face and sat beside the stream. He made no effort to follow them as they walked around the rock.

Twelve

Under the Lake

C url led the way to the rough side of the rock, to the very place she'd scrambled down weeks ago.

Ploddin went up after her, followed by Lacht, who deliberately went last in case Ploddin needed a boost, but the young blacksmith pulled his good leg up from one foothold to another without any problem. *No need to worry!*

She climbed the rock after him, smiling as she imagined the expression on Ploddin's face if he knew how often she worried over his leg. *Sourplum, definitely sourplum.* She was still smiling when she reached the top of the rock and found herself on the brink of Wasso Lake.

Abruptly, she quit smiling.

Sunset had passed, and the evening mists swirled up from the surface of the lake to twist and turn about their legs like happy cats. Lacht looked sideways at Ploddin.

He wasn't smiling either.

Not long ago, not long ago at all, the two of them had avoided Wasso Lake with a passion. Then they'd had to walk into that awful pond.

"Come on," Curl urged them and stepped forward into the water.

Ploddin lifted a hand toward Lacht, and she took it gratefully. Together, they followed Curl into the mists that swirled over them, into the water that didn't feel wet, until their heads went under the surface and the pale gold of Wasso Lake surrounded them.

A confusing jumble of rocks crowded the underwater slope on this side of the lake, but Curl confidently weaved her way through them, bouncing with excitement the whole way.

It was when the rocky slope leveled out into an open smoothness that extended on and on, as far as they could see, that the Wassandra girl sank onto the golden floor and put her head on her arms.

"I've got to rest," she whispered shakily. "I'm tired."

"You need to get home," Ploddin said gruffly, kneeling beside her. "Your parents will know what to do for you."

Lacht's heart clinched. She knew Ploddin's gruffness didn't come from crossness, not this time. What had all the weeks of hunger and fear done to Curl?

"Point me in the right direction," Lacht urged. "You don't need to take me. You should go straight to your home."

"No," Curl objected. "Some places in Wasso Lake can get you into trouble. I know!" Even in her weakness, she grinned at them.

"I bet you do," Ploddin told her, grinning back. "Let me carry you again."

He picked her up, and she draped her arms about his neck and lay her head on his shoulder.

"That way," she said, pointing with a long, graceful finger, and off they went, walking through the deepest part of the lake.

The water didn't darken in the deep places of Wasso Lake; it just became a more intense gold. No one spoke. Quiet surrounded and filled them, a deep quiet that they didn't want to disturb.

They walked forty more minutes, with Curl directing them by waves of her graceful hands. When they started a gradual climb, Ploddin finally broke the silence.

"I wonder what it's like down here during the middle of the day," he said.

"It's lighter," Curl told him and yawned a very loud yawn.

Lacht yawned too. She still felt hungry, only she was thirsty now as well. *Hmmm.*

Discreetly turning her head to one side, she started gulping. The water didn't have a taste, but it certainly relieved her thirst and—

"What are you doing?" Ploddin asked, smiling widely. "You look exactly like a fish with long black hair!"

Lacht broke into laughter.

She'd never laughed underwater. It caused ripples, golden ripples that undulated out from her. Up to now, she'd only seen the tops of ripples, tops that made irregular waves on the surface of a pond, waves that ended with splashes against the shoreline. The underwater ripples waved from side to side in tight little oblongs. The further away they got, the bigger the oblongs grew, until in the distance the water rolled in long ovals that began to lose their shape.

"Poppa used to tell me that the mists of Wasso Lake came from our laughter," Curl remarked from the comfort of Ploddin's arms. "Every time we laughed, it traveled through the water until it reached the surface, where it changed into mist and jumped for joy. He said that was why the mists swirled. I believed him when I was a child."

Lacht smiled at her. "Then I'm glad I look like a fish when I drink. I make more mists!"

"Drink!" Ploddin exclaimed. "Why didn't you tell me we could drink this water? When I've been about to die of—"

"Like this," Lacht interrupted him.

She demonstrated.

Ploddin opened his mouth and started gulping. Curl shouted with laughter, and Lacht giggled helplessly herself. He did look like a fish; a big fish with short black hair that stood on end and waved back and forth in the golden water.

The laugh ripples rushed out in long, swaying ovals as he winked at the two girls and kept on drinking, mouth opening and closing in round *O*'s.

The Wassandra made no sound as they approached. Curl straightened up in Ploddin's arms right before they arrived and called out, but Lacht couldn't tell what had alerted the girl.

All at once, tall, willowy forms stood in front of them; and Curl was weeping, leaning out from Ploddin with her arms stretched towards one of them. With a graceful bound, the Wassandra man leaped to her side and gathered her to him.

Singing filled the water then; male voices blending in a harmony so beautiful that Lacht could only stare, eyes wide. When the singing stopped, she heard an answering song, far off and barely discernible, but beautiful all the same.

Curl still sobbed, clutching at her father's neck. He was crying too, and Lacht didn't even try to stop her own tears, but she smiled as she cried. At least she smiled until she noticed the faces of the other men in the search party. Still and emotionless, the men watched Lacht and Ploddin. Their eyes didn't waver, and their expressions didn't change.

Abruptly, Lacht's lips straightened. She was tired of stop-and-start smiling, but she couldn't help it.

They don't know, she realized, *who we are. They haven't seen Wet Ones in years, and, for all they know, we sneaked into their lake and kidnapped their girl.*

"Curl," she whispered nervously.

The girl sobbed louder.

"Curl," Lacht insisted, "you need to tell your people that we're friends!"

Helplessly, Curl waved one hand above her head. She couldn't speak, but she did start making an effort to control her sobs.

The men waited silently, their tall golden forms at home in the water. The short, brown curls on their heads bobbed gently in the underwater currents, but everything else about them suggested flowing grace.

Lacht tried another smile but knew immediately that it was a mistake and took it off her face. Ploddin reached over and held her hand again.

116

"It's all right," he told her. "They'll understand in a minute."

The sobbing girl hiccupped loudly, and Lacht watched the effect of the hiccup on the water. It made more of a bumping effect than anything else, little bumps of water movement that moved away in bigger and bigger bumps.

"Poppa," Curl finally said, "I'm sorry. I'm so sorry! I ran away and followed a stream that falls over a gray rock outside the lake. I knew you wouldn't think to follow me there, because nobody else would dream of leaving Wasso Lake. The stream emptied into a golden pond, and I wanted to see inside it."

Curl had sounded shaky up to this point, but her words got much shakier now. Lacht could barely understand them.

"I found, I found a Wert under there!"

The men started, and Curl's father clutched her closer.

"It was horrible with all those arms, and I was frightened, but I saw a panotka plant and hid in its leaves. The Wert couldn't catch me, but I couldn't get out either. I tried and tried, but it always chased me back. Then Keshua came and told me Lacht would come, and then Lacht came."

Curl took a deep breath.

"That's Lacht," she said, pointing. "She stayed with me until the Wert started through the leaves, because they'd all turned purple, and most of them had fallen. We had to run for it, but the Wert would have gotten us if Ploddin hadn't jumped in between us.

"That's Ploddin," she said with another point. "He killed the Wert. He's a hero!"

Everyone stared at Ploddin, who cleared his throat and turned as red as the coals in his forge.

"Thank you for saving my daughter," Curl's father said to Ploddin and Lacht in a rich baritone. He bowed his head as he added, "We honor you."

The tall, golden bodies of the men swayed as they all lowered their heads before Lacht and Ploddin.

"No, don't," Lacht blurted out. "I kept having dreams, and I know now that the Plete sent them, but I didn't want to be a Wet One, and I didn't want to go into that pond, even though I knew Curl was there. Keshua almost had to pull me into the water."

"I spent twenty years refusing to tell anyone I was a Wet One," Ploddin admitted in his turn, "and I didn't believe anything Lacht had told me until she'd been gone for hours. If Brownie hadn't led me to them, I would never have reached the girls in time."

"We should honor Brownie then?" asked one of the men.

Curl waved both hands above her head, as she shouted her agreement, "Yes! Let's honor Brownie!"

Lacht and Ploddin laughed at her, and the men shook their heads in confusion.

Ploddin explained, "Brownie is a dog, an animal that lives above the water. I think the only one you should honor is Keshua."

"Keshua has obviously played the major role in saving our girl," answered Curl's father with a smile, "but you have both done your parts. You, Lacht, comforted my daughter; and you, Ploddin, killed the Wert. We will not forget."

"Poppa," whispered Curl, slumping against her father after the momentary burst of energy, "I want to see Mama."

"You shall," he said. "All else must wait. Wave will direct your friends to Burkin Village, and I will take you home."

He started to leave, but Curl stopped him.

"Wait, Poppa," she said. "Wait a minute."

She looked at Lacht and Ploddin, and the brown flecks in her beautiful, golden eyes did not jump sideways this time.

"I will see you soon," she told them. "I love you."

"We love you too," answered Lacht, and her throat tightened as much as the first time she'd responded to those words from the girl. "Go home and get well."

"Poppa," Curl said again, and the tall man bent his head to hear her whisper.

"My daughter tells me that you have a hurt leg," he remarked, straightening and turning to Ploddin.

118

"Well, yes," Ploddin answered shortly.

Don't be rude, Lacht begged him in her mind.

"We have a healer skilled in such things," the tall Wassandra announced simply. "If you come with us, we will ask him to help you."

Lacht tensed.

Hey! I don't want to go home alone. Tell them no, Ploddin. Muster up a little rudeness and tell them no.

Then she saw his face.

"Perhaps I should wait," he said evenly. "Lacht doesn't want to return home by herself."

"No," she insisted sharply. "Go with them, Ploddin. I'll be fine."

He started to say something, but she interrupted him before he could start. "Just go. See the Wassandra healer."

She had meant to say it more graciously, but at least her sincerity must have showed. Ploddin nodded. Then he leaned forward and kissed her cheek.

That perked Curl up. "Oh, ho ho! Did you see that?"

The eleven-year-old girl chortled her delight, and the Wassandra men all smiled. Lacht wanted to hide, but she didn't have anywhere to go. She turned sunset pink instead and stared at the floor of the lake.

"Don't stay long," she told the sand.

"We will come to Burkin Village tomorrow when the sun is high," Curl's father assured her.

Then they moved off, and Ploddin moved with them. He waved once at Lacht before disappearing in the golden distance. She swallowed hard and smiled at the tall young man who had stayed with her. Curl's father had called him Wave.

"Follow me," Wave said in a deep bass. "I will guide you home."

They walked for ten minutes up the gentle slope. Lacht went slowly, thinking over all that had happened and watching the ground, which was turning sandy. The last time she'd seen that sandy slope, she'd sat at its top, just inside the lake, and accepted the fact that she was a Wet One.

That was just last night, she thought, shaking her head.

A shadow on the sand interrupted her reverie on the passage of time. She glanced up and saw a thick wooden pole to their left, firmly embedded in the sand. Short boards intersected the long pole at regular intervals as if to form a ladder.

She stopped walking and her arms hugged each other. What strange Wassandra construction was this? Another wooden pole, just as thick as the first one, but without the short boards, stood five feet to the side of the first one. Ahead of her, other pairs of poles rose out of the sand. None of them had the short boards either.

The poles were connected by some sort of flat roof, but she couldn't see it very clearly. She could see the poles easily enough, even the far ones, but the narrow roof stayed vague even when she squinted. Why couldn't she see it better?

Later, Lacht marveled at how long it took her to figure out the obvious answer. However, this was the first time she'd stood on the bottom of a golden lake and tried to see above it.

"The pier," she announced suddenly. "I'm seeing underneath the pier. I know where I am now," she added, turning to her guide, who had paused when she did and waited quietly.

"You can go home. I'm sure you don't want to miss all the celebration."

"I will stay with you until you leave Wasso Lake," Wave answered in his deep, melodious voice. His long arms gestured as if playing an accompaniment to his words. "You helped my cousin in her time of trouble. I will not leave you until you stand again on Stalli land."

She smiled up at him. "Curl's your cousin?"

"A distant cousin, but a close friend." He motioned her forward.

They walked past three pairs of wooden poles before Lacht's head followed Wave's through the surface of the lake. She blinked

120

at the swirling mists above them and wanted to pause again, but Wave kept walking up the slope into the mists. He didn't stop until she had stepped out of the water entirely onto the meadow's grass.

"You are safe now?" he questioned.

"Yes, yes, I'm fine," she answered, wishing yet again that her family's cottage bordered the lake.

"I will say good-bye until high sun tomorrow," Wave said and turned.

A minute later, he had walked under the mists and beneath the surface of Wasso Lake.

Lacht took a deep breath.

I'm not going to like the rest of this night.

She straightened a dry skirt and brushed back dry hair. The mists swirled around her, and she waved a hand through them. How pretty they were!

"I'm delaying again," she whispered, sighing heavily as she made herself turn.

The night air darkened with each step away from Wasso Lake. After ten steps, Lacht could only see the outline of grass, not its color.

"Who is it?" queried a low voice when she reached the road.

Meddy was sitting on the porch of her cottage. Lacht crossed the village road, climbed the porch steps, and stood before her.

"Where have you been, Lacht? Is Ploddin here too?"

Lacht stood without answering, feeling stupid, and wondering where to begin.

"Come inside," the older woman urged. "You're exhausted."

"I need to get home," began Lacht. "Need to—"

Several voices interrupted her. A noisy group of people had started down the road toward them.

"Oh no," she moaned, shrinking toward Meddy.

"Come in, quick!" Meddy ordered, taking charge.

They entered the cottage without anyone from the group seeing them, and Meddy made Lacht sit at the kitchen table.

"Ploddin's all right," Lacht told her, slumping against the back of her chair. "He's with the Wassandra. They're going to fix his leg."

The Stalli woman grabbed at the tabletop and sat heavily in the nearest chair. Her face stiffened, and one eye twitched. "Ploddin is with the Wassandra?"

"Yes, he and I are Wet Ones, and we rescued the missing Wassandra girl," Lacht said in a rush.

How would Meddy take all this?

"Ploddin is a Wet One?" Meddy repeated. "He's with the Wassandra?"

Lacht nodded dumbly. She'd have to tell the whole story soon, but she didn't want to do it now. Fortunately, Meddy didn't ask for more details. Her eyes studied Lacht intently, then she relaxed. A half grin lifted one side of her mouth.

"I want to see Crispin's face when he hears this!"

"I don't," muttered Lacht.

"Meddy," someone shouted from outside the front door, "any news from Ploddin?"

Lacht stiffened. She looked at Meddy, begging as hard as she could without saying anything.

"Go down the hall and out the back door in case they come in," instructed her friend quietly. "Stay under the trees."

As Meddy shouted out the front window, "I haven't talked to Ploddin since yesterday." Lacht slipped silently down the hall and into the yard.

When the group of people had left, Meddy stuck her head out the door. "Good, you're still here," she whispered. "Moben walked up with that group. He'll take you home."

Moben, Meddy's quiet husband, stepped outside and stood in front of Lacht, who wanted to yawn in his face but didn't. She'd met Moben, but she didn't really know him, and she wished she could go home by herself.

"Ploddin is with the Wassandra?" he whispered.

Meddy had obviously done some fast explaining.

"Yes," she said.

122

A smile grew on the Stalli man's face until she lost sight of its ends. Presumably, it went under his hair and met in the back of his head. Tired as she was, she couldn't help but smile back. Moben chuckled deeply, but quietly.

Then he whispered, "I want to see Crispin's face when he finds out!"

"I don't," repeated Lacht, but her lips curved upward again in her last smile of the night.

Moben managed to get her halfway home without meeting anyone by taking shortcuts through people's yards and crossing roads at dark places. However, a crowd of people rushed rapidly around a corner and spotted them before they could take cover.

"Lacht!" someone shouted. "Here's Lacht! She's all right. Spread the word!"

The whole town escorted her the rest of the way home—at least she felt as if it did. Crispin walked next to her, holding her arm as if she might collapse without his support. One of the wise ones of Burkin Village, an older man named Matushin, walked on her other side.

"Where have you been?" Matushin asked her.

"Wait 'til I get home," she answered, nodding twice to signify she had something important to say.

The news of her arrival reached her cottage before she did. Her family erupted down the porch steps and into the road, running to greet her. Frenne was crying; Winnel was beaming; Irsht was talking nonstop.

"Lacht, we looked for you everywhere! I even checked the path toward the desert, thinking you might have gotten homesick for the Root Forest."

"That's crazy," Lacht said, trying not to yawn. Her stomach growled unhappily.

"Come in," Frenne invited everyone as they reached the door of the cottage.

To Lacht's relief, most people turned Frenne down. Only Matushin stayed. The other wise one of Burkin Village, a man with the unlikely name of Bleek, met them with a welcoming smile in the sitting room.

Crispin and a few others stayed too. Lacht wished they hadn't. She felt too tired for what she knew was coming. Her stomach growled again.

"This day has made me realize how bad those Wassandra parents must feel," Frenne said, shaking her head as she sank weakly onto their small sofa.

"You're right," Winnel agreed, sitting next to her and putting an arm around her shoulders. "We lost a daughter for a day; their daughter's been gone for weeks!"

"Not anymore," Lacht whispered.

Nobody heard her.

"They found the Wassandra girl," she said a little louder.

That time they heard her.

"How do you know?" several people asked at the same time.

"Because I'm a Wet One and so is Ploddin, and we rescued her. Can I have something to eat?"

Thirteen

The Morning After

Lacht woke up early the next morning—too early.

She turned to her left side and tried to go back to sleep. When that didn't work, she turned to her right side and let her head sink deeply into the pillow, but the new position squashed her right ear. Punching a hole in the pillow without opening her eyes, she tried again.

The right side didn't work either. After the second wake-up yawn, she gave up and gazed out the clean bedroom window. A fingernail-sized piece of smudge sat smugly in a lower corner. How had she missed it?

I need to scrape that, she thought and hoped it was on the inside of the window and not the outside. When she heard someone climbing the steps onto the porch, Lacht grimaced. Crispin must have arrived.

Last night, after her startling announcement, the wise ones had hustled everyone out of the cottage except for Lacht's family. Then they'd insisted on listening to her story straight through, without any questions from anyone.

Crispin had protested. His brother was still missing, and from what he understood before Matushin escorted him to the door, Ploddin had remained under Wasso Lake. This was not news to make Crispin happy. Lacht had known he'd come back the next morning, but she hadn't known he'd arrive before breakfast.

She got up and dressed, wondering whether Meddy and

Moben had enjoyed Crispin's reaction. She certainly hadn't. Walking quietly down the short hallway toward the kitchen, her stomach made a familiar rumble, and she sniffed.

Ummm, scrambled eggs and toast.

Peeking through the doorway, she grimaced again. Frenne had sat Crispin at the table and put a plate of eggs and toast in front of him.

Where was Irsht? She could handle Crispin. One strong personality needed to be matched by another one. Lacht put what she hoped was a strong expression on her face and inched into the kitchen.

"Hi!" she said weakly.

Crispin jumped up so quickly his chair fell over backwards. "Lacht, where's my brother?"

"I told you last night," she said, sitting at her place and staring hopefully at her mother.

Their breakfast guest creased his face into sour lines worthy of Ploddin. "He should have returned by now. Are you sure he's all right?"

"Yes," she answered shortly. She didn't look forward to telling Crispin her story. He wouldn't like it. "Mom, I need to eat."

"All right," Frenne said, answering her daughter's unspoken plea as well as the spoken one. "No more questions, Crispin, until Lacht has had breakfast. You may as well eat too."

"I'm not hungry," he grumbled, but he picked up the chair and sat in front of his plate again.

Lacht counted inside her head. When the young man across the table shrugged and reached for his fork, she said brightly, "Six seconds!"

"What?" he asked. He didn't frown again, but he came close.

"You took six seconds to decide to eat. Fastest fork lifter in Stalli!" she reminded him.

Instead of the smile she'd hoped for, Crispin put down his fork and glared at her. She'd never seen him glare before.

"Lacht, I'm worried Ploddin's trapped under that lake. You

126

say he's fine, but how do you know? The wise ones should have let me stay last night and hear the whole story, but since they didn't, I want to hear it now."

She swallowed a bite of egg on top of buttered toast. "I know you have a right to hear my story, Crispin, but I don't think you'll change your mind after you've heard it. You're too prejudiced."

He jumped as if she'd thrown something at him. "I am not prejudiced," he insisted.

"Are so!" stated an opinionated voice from the porch.

Lacht smiled with relief at the sight of her little sister, who strode into the kitchen and stood, hands on hips, fixing the young man with a schoolteacher stare.

"You are so prejudiced that if I was Lacht I wouldn't tell you a word," Irsht continued.

"I am not—" He began again to defend himself, but he didn't have a chance, not with Irsht in her present mood.

"Ever since we met you," she interrupted loudly, "you've told us scary stories about Wassandra and Wet Ones. Now it turns out that Lacht and your own brother are Wet Ones, and you can't accept it. You don't really believe all those stories you made up, do you?"

Crispin turned to Frenne for help and saw Winnel standing quietly beside his wife. He must have come in with Irsht. There was no help from that direction then. He knew what Winnel thought about his stories.

Crispin stayed quiet for a minute, which gave Lacht enough time to finish her breakfast, washing down the last few bites with hot tea.

"I did make up some stories," he finally said with a dignity that surprised her. "I'm sorry for that, but I don't know why I should trust a strange people who have avoided Burkin Village for years. We couldn't go under the water after the Wassandra. They chose not to come out to see us." He turned toward Irscht. "If Ploddin had told you Lacht was under the lake," he asked her, "wouldn't you worry?"

"Maybe," she admitted, "but I'd believe Ploddin better than you're believing Lacht."

"I'm through eating," Lacht announced. "Let me tell you the story, Crispin. You don't know what a hero Ploddin is."

She'd chosen the right words. Crispin brightened up considerably, which made it easier for her to start. When she got to the part in which Ploddin leapt between the two girls and the Wert, Crispin jumped up from his chair, knocking it down again behind him. "That's the way," he cheered on his brother. "Carve that monster to pieces, Ploddin!"

Lacht's face brightened. Maybe this would turn out better than she'd expected. She continued her story, but when Ploddin walked off across the bottom of the lake to see the Wassandra healer, Crispin's eyes narrowed.

"Stalli healers have taken care of my brother," he told her severely. "Why would he need a Wassandra one?"

"The Wassandra might know something different," she answered him wearily.

She was tired already of telling her story, and she knew she'd be telling it the rest of her life. Maybe she was just tired.

"Here's another cup of tea," Frenne said, handing her a cup of fragrant tea. The steam smelled like honey. Lacht took the cup gratefully and started sipping.

"Everything will be cleared up today at noon, when the Wassandra come out of Wasso Lake," Winnel pointed out.

"*If* they come out," Crispin muttered, and Irsht frowned at him. "Well, what will we do if they don't?" he asked, throwing his hands out to either side.

Lacht sighed. "If something holds them up, which I don't think will happen, then I'll walk into the lake and find out what's going on."

Irsht and Frenne stiffened, and Crispin nodded at them.

"You see what it feels like," he said, rising to leave.

"We'll meet you near the dock at noon," Winnel said, trying to bolster the young man's spirits.

128

/// /// ///

People gathered well before noon. The entire village came, of course, plus people from two nearby villages. News of that magnitude traveled fast through the mountains, and anyone who could possibly get to Burkin Village by noon did so.

Lacht and her family arrived an hour early and sat with the wise ones on the grassy meadow, thirty feet up from the water's edge. They were the only ones with chairs. Some people had brought quilts to spread on the meadow, but most planned to sit right on top of the grass. Nobody worried about grass stains, not today! Besides, who wanted to sit?

The excited Stallis mulled about, chatting and calling to each other. None of them ventured any closer to the water than the wise ones, though. They wanted to see the strange people from under the lake, but they also wanted to keep a safe distance away.

Lacht watched the crowd gather and tried to spot the woman who had given her a cinnamon bun. She wanted to thank her again.

"Who are you looking for?" Irsht finally asked, after her sister had stood up four times and surveyed the crowd.

"That woman who gave me a cinnamon bun," she answered, craning her neck in yet another direction. "Her husband's name is Hanri, and she lives on the edge of town. I don't believe she told me her name."

One of the wise ones cleared his throat. "Lacht," he said and then hesitated.

Sitting in her chair again, Lacht turned to him expectantly. Bleek contemplated her with a strange expression. "No one of that description lives in Burkin Village," he told her gently.

"Nobody here is named Hanri," Matushin backed him up.

Lacht stared, bewildered, at the two of them. "I don't understand. The woman gave me a cinnamon bun."

"Cinnamon is something Paigens harvest," Winnel, who seemed to know what was going on, reminded her, "in the

129

southern marshes of Tarth. You had it growing up because the Root Forest borders the Paigen marshes, and Root people trade regularly with Paigens. No one in Burkin Village has had cinnamon for years."

"I ate a cinnamon bun," she insisted. "It was delicious—the best I've ever had."

"I have no doubt about that," Matushin assured her solemnly. "Keshua would have given you the best."

When his daughter continued to look bewildered, Winnel explained to her slowly, as if he found it too big for words himself. "We think Keshua sent one of his messengers to encourage and strengthen you before you left Burkin Village. The woman gave you a cinnamon bun because he knew you'd like it. She talked to you and helped you relax; then she let you go."

Lacht shook her head. "She was fat," she protested, as if Keshua couldn't possibly have fat messengers.

Winnel frowned slightly. "What does that have to do with it? No doubt, Keshua designed her appearance to put you at your ease."

"But I drank from a well," she continued to protest. "The cottage was right behind it. If that woman and Hanri don't live there, who does?"

"Tell us again where you stopped," Bleek suggested.

She tried, but she didn't know how to explain yesterday's run through the back village roads and finally gave up. "I could retrace my route easier than talk about it... at least I think I could," she added a little less assuredly.

"That's a good idea," agreed Matushin. "Later today, we'll follow you to the place Keshua met you."

"It wasn't Keshua," Lacht reminded him, and her lower lip quivered slightly. "He came to Curl, but he didn't come to me."

"He will, one day," Bleek told her and nodded sympathetically. "I yearn to see him too. At least, you've met one of his messengers. Most people don't get that!"

"Oh, I don't know," Matushin said cheerfully. "We might

meet his messengers every day and not recognize them. I had my suspicions about Winnel when I first met him."

Winnel snorted, and the three men started sharing stories they'd heard about Keshua's messengers. Lacht listened, shaking her head at the thought of anything that special happening to her.

A disturbance in the crowd made them all turn its way, though they couldn't see anything from their chairs. Lacht stood and craned her neck again, but she still couldn't see anything. She could hear it, though. The sound of heavy footsteps got louder, and her eyes narrowed.

Less than a minute later, a large group of young men with hard eyes and set features pushed to the front of the crowd. Each of the young men carried a heavy wooden stick. Crispin, of course, led them. He held two sticks, one in each hand.

Lacht scowled. "Put those sticks down!" she said, her words so hot with anger they could have scalded water.

"We don't intend to use them unless we have to," Crispin answered grimly.

Bleek and Matushin began to push themselves out of their chairs. As wise ones of Burkin Village, they had a great deal of authority. Bleek cleared his throat, preparatory to issuing a command, but Lacht beat him to it.

"I don't care what you intend. I want the sticks on the ground, and I mean now. Otherwise, I will go into Wasso Lake and tell the Wassandra that the meeting is canceled."

Bleek and Matushin stopped halfway out of their chairs. They glanced at each other, then sat back down.

Lacht glared at Crispin, who stood very still.

"If there's trouble," he started to say.

"There's not going to be any trouble except what I'm having right now with you," she thundered. "Drop those sticks, or I'll break one over your head. I mean it, Crispin!"

The young Stalli men stared at the slim girl who was threatening their leader, and the grim expressions passed from their faces. Several of them grinned. Slowly, Crispin released his hold on the two sticks, and they fell to the ground beside him.

Lacht transferred her glare to the men on either side of Crispin. Quickly, they dropped their sticks. The crowd stayed silent, which made it possible to hear the soft thudding of sticks falling in various places all over the meadow. Obviously, other people had anticipated trouble too.

Clapping hands interrupted the silence. Quiet Moben clapped from where he stood in the crowd, giving Lacht support and lightening everyone's mood. Moben didn't say anything. He just clapped, and his big smile spread around his head again.

Other people started clapping then, and Lacht's shoulders sagged a full inch. When Meddy pushed through the crowd to stand beside her, she leaned against the older woman gratefully.

"It's noon," Winnel announced.

Lacht straightened up and looked toward the lake, a whole meadowful of people looking with her. Wasso Lake's golden mists had retreated underneath the water, as they always did that time of day. The lake rippled gently with their movements.

Suddenly, a dozen heads broke the surface of the water on one side of the pier. The crowd gasped, and one woman cried out in fear but was quickly hushed. Lacht smiled with relief. Her eyes started to fill.

Stop it, she told herself furiously and bullied the tears back inside her eyes. *I want to see this.*

The heads moved toward the shore, and the waiting Stallis could see their light brown curls now. Curls were all right. Curls were not threatening, but as the Wassandra came closer, their long arms and fingers and their unusual height became apparent.

None of the Stallis moved. None of them said anything. *What a picture this would make,* Lacht thought and bullied more tears back.

The tall Wassandra with their golden clothing walked gracefully out of the gold water onto the blue grass, where Stallis waited in their blue clothing; both peoples framed on either side by blue-leafed trees beginning to turn purple, and everything—

132

people, water, and trees arched over by Tarth's great, purple sky.

This time a squeal interrupted the silence, as a small body ran through the ranks of Wassandra and hurled itself toward Lacht.

"I'm here, Lacht," Curl shouted. "I told you I'd come! Did you bring me a blueberry pie and cinnamon bun?"

Stallis loved children. Without a doubt, before them raced the missing child Lacht and Ploddin had found. Smiles spread over the waiting crowd; and the approaching Wassandra, whose faces had resembled the shaded side of a granite cliff, returned them.

Lacht ran forward to meet Curl, and the girls hugged each other tightly.

"Have you found a Wet One my age?" asked Curl in a piercing whisper that carried easily to the upper edge of the meadow. "One I can marry, you know."

"Don't talk about that," Lacht hastily told her. "You're too young to think about marriage!"

"You're not," Curl whispered, hopping up and down.

Lacht wondered helplessly how an eleven-year-old girl could whisper that loudly.

"Curl!" a rich, soprano scolded, and Curl quit hopping.

Lacht glanced up quickly. A tall woman stood in front of her, smiling.

"Thank you, Lacht, for saving my baby," Curl's mother said, and her words sang with emotion.

She could give concerts, just talking.

"You, you're welcome," Lacht stammered.

Curl's mother wore a pale gold dress with a brown cord wrapped loosely around her waist. Her long arms and fingers moved gracefully in the air whenever she spoke, and the light brown curls on her head glimmered with golden highlights. Her golden eyes shone bright with feeling.

"Mama?" Curl whispered frantically and beckoned.

Her mother leaned towards her tenderly.

"Don't call me a baby," Curl begged.

The woman glanced toward Lacht, then back at her daughter.

"I will not call you a baby, if you will not embarrass your friend further," she said in an uncompromising tone.

"Deal," agreed Curl, and Lacht laughed happily.

"I'll let you know if she slips," she told Curl's mother.

The woman stood up again and smiled, but her eyes glistened with unshed tears. One hand moved toward Lacht's face, and a gentle finger stroked her cheek. "Thank you," she said again.

"Keshua sent me," Lacht felt compelled to explain.

"I know, but you went."

A slightly hoarse, yet determined voice interrupted them. "Where's Ploddin?" Crispin asked.

Lacht spun around, then didn't know whether to roll her eyes or smile.

Crispin alone, out of all the crowd of Stallis, had summoned up the courage to approach the Wassandra group waiting behind Curl and her mother. Crispin had walked across the blue grass to ask about his brother. He hadn't even picked up his sticks.

"Ploddin is coming," one of the men answered in a deep intonation that could have passed for a well-tuned cello. "Our healer treated and bound his leg, then arranged for two Wassandra to carry him on an invalid mat across the lake. They must walk slowly to avoid jostling the hurt leg. Curl's father and our aged ones are walking beside him. We could honor him no higher."

"Curl wanted to hurry, and I would not let her go alone," Curl's mother explained. "We came ahead, but the others should arrive within the hour."

Crispin looked at the beautiful Wassandra woman and, for once in his life, words failed him.

Words did not fail Curl. "Is that Ploddin's brother?" she asked Lacht with great interest. "Is he the one who made up stories about us?"

Before Lacht could answer, and even before Crispin could clear his throat in embarrassment, Curl added, "He is *so* handsome! Are you married?"

"Curl!" scolded her mother again.

134

Crispin grinned. "That's all right," he told Curl's mother, then turned to Curl. "No, I'm not married. Are you proposing?"

"Yes!" shouted Curl.

"No!" scolded her mother, and as the listening Stallis and Wassandra laughed, the last vestiges of fear and suspicion vanished from their faces.

Fourteen

Winnel Takes Action

When Ploddin and his group emerged from the water thirty minutes later, they found Wassandra and Stalli scattered over the meadow, talking and smiling at each other.

"Well, well," remarked Ploddin. "I thought we'd have more trouble than this getting to know each other."

"Trouble?" Crispin responded, smiling brightly at his brother. "How could two of Keshua's peoples have trouble between them?"

"I can't imagine," Ploddin answered dryly.

Lacht opened her mouth, but Crispin hastily spoke before she could.

"What did they do to your leg?" he asked. "Did they help it?"

"We won't know the results until the binding comes off," Ploddin told him, "but their healer did plenty to it beforehand! It hasn't hurt this much since the day of the accident!"

"Oh no," Lacht said, wringing her hands together. "I'm sorry. I, I'm sure the healer meant to help."

Crispin had started scowling again, and she didn't want him to speak the ugly thoughts she could see in his eyes.

"What exactly did he do?" she asked.

"He prodded and poked and stretched and pulled until I wanted to scream," Ploddin answered, shuddering at the memory but otherwise smiling cheerfully enough.

Neither Lacht nor Crispin smiled back.

"Blow needed to understand the extent of your injury before he could decide what to do," a nearby Wassandra man explained in words that sounded like notes from a perfectly pitched viola. "He is very skilled at his craft."

"I wanted to relocate Blow's nose to the other side of his head," Ploddin told him, "not that I'm arguing. I don't doubt what you're saying, but I wanted to punch him all the same. Unfortunately, he moved out of reach, and I lost my chance."

The tall man nodded. "I understand. When I was ten years old, Blow treated me for a broken ankle. I kicked him twice with the uninjured foot before he shackled it down. Nevertheless, my ankle healed completely. Perhaps you will have the same good results with your leg."

"What did he do?" asked Lacht again. She still wasn't smiling, and she wanted details.

"He wrapped underwater leaves around my leg," Ploddin explained. "They were red like panotka leaves though not as long, and they made my leg feel hot. I mean metal-in-a-forge hot. Feverish doesn't begin to describe it. Right about the time I'd decided to wrap those leaves around Blow's head, he cut them off and started pulling.

"I reminded him that Stalli legs don't grow as long as Wassandra legs. It was an important fact that he had obviously forgotten, so I reminded him of it several times, but he ignored me and kept pulling. I thought he meant to pull the leg right off my body."

A little audience of Wassandra had gathered around Ploddin. They laughed with evident appreciation.

"Blow is a good healer, but his manners do need improvement," one of the women remarked in a striking alto.

"I am surprised he is still alive after mauling so many people," another alto commented, "but he is a good healer!"

"After he'd stretched my leg to twice its normal length," Ploddin continued, "he strapped it to a frame. Then he covered both frame and leg with cloth, wrapped the cloth with a thin layer of those red leaves, and put a binding around the whole thing."

"Does your leg feel hot now?" asked Crispin, walking to one side and staring suspiciously at the bound leg.

"Not like before," Ploddin assured him. "I may sweat more than normal this week, however; and I do not want to do any blacksmithing!"

Lacht had walked to the other side.

"The Wassandra healer didn't stretch your leg twice as long as normal," she informed Ploddin. "It's still the same length."

"Lacht!" he commented, closing his eyes and lifting his face up to the violet sky with a prolonged sigh, "don't you know a hyperbole when you hear it?"

"He is not exaggerating about everything," one of the Wassandra tenors defended Ploddin. "Blow will help you, but in his own way."

Lacht smiled at Ploddin. "Well, I'm glad you're here anyway."

"And you aren't even wet," Crispin marveled for the seventh time. "I saw you come out of the water, and you aren't wet anywhere, not even your clothes."

"Yep, that's why they call us Wet Ones," his brother remarked placidly.

"Why—" Crispin began the obvious question, but Lacht had to leave then.

The wise ones of Burkin Village and the aged ones of Wasso Lake had sent for her.

♫ ♫ ♫

"I like your name better than ours," one of the aged ones was booming in deep-bell reverberations as Lacht walked up to them. "'Aged ones' always makes me feel old—and I am only 119!"

"You must live longer than we do," Bleek responded with interest, but then he saw the Stalli girl.

"Lacht, we wondered if you'd take us to the place where you

met Keshua's messenger. Splash and Drip want to see it too."

"Of course," she agreed and moved off at the side of one of the tall Wassandra men. "Are you Splash or Drip?"

"I am Drip, unfortunately," he responded, melodiously baritone. "My parents loved the sound rain makes as it falls into the lake. They failed to realize that the word might prove less than desirable as a name!"

Drip had a good sense of humor. He kept Lacht entertained all the way to Ploddin and Crispin's home. Then she asked everyone to quit talking.

Staring at the road, she concentrated on remembering. When she'd run away furious at Ploddin, she'd gone around that corner to begin with, then she'd charged down this road, and turned somewhere. She paused in sudden doubt but remembered an overhanging branch from an apple tree.

"I went around the apple tree," she murmured. "Then I turned again here and, for no reason that I can remember, cut across this yard. When the road ended, I was out of breath, so I stopped right beyond this big oak tree and leaned on the gate."

She stopped on the other side of the oak tree. The others, a little out of breath themselves, stopped behind her. There was no gate. There was no well. There wasn't even a cottage.

They stood in front of an empty yard. The forest crowded in on one side, making the yard smaller than normal. No one had chosen to build a home there.

Lacht stared intently in front of her as if she could make the things she remembered materialize if she looked hard enough. Small bumps appeared on her skin, and she shivered.

Matushin put an arm around her shoulders. "This is the place?" he asked to make sure.

She nodded.

"Things were here before," she insisted shakily. "I touched them. I, I drank from a well right inside the, the gate."

The four men transferred their attention from the empty yard to the trembling girl.

"You say the woman gave you a cinnamon bun?" Bleek asked, as if he didn't know the answer.

"Yes, right out of the oven, or that's what she said. It, it warmed my hands."

"The bun tasted good, did it, or only fair?" someone questioned.

She didn't notice who had spoken.

"It was delicious!" she responded forcefully. "The cinnamon and sugar and butter ran together the way I like them to, and the bread part was good enough to enjoy all by itself!"

"The water from the well refreshed you?" chimed in Splash with what seemed great curiosity.

"Oh yes, it was wonderfully cold."

The old men stopped asking questions then, but they'd helped Lacht remember the good things she had enjoyed. She stopped trembling, and the bumps on her skin went away.

"Well, we can't do anything about cinnamon buns, but I think this would make an excellent place to dig a well," Matushin finally suggested. "I suspect the water here would taste unusually fresh."

"You are right," Drip agreed.

"I haven't given up on cinnamon buns," Bleek argued. "Let's send someone to the Paigen marshes this fall. I haven't tasted cinnamon since I was a child."

"We'll have it all then," Matushin announced heartily.

"Except for that woman," remarked Lacht, whose spirits had risen. "She was nice; I liked her a lot. Do you really think she was a messenger of Keshua's?"

"Yes!" all the men stated in loud unison; then they smiled at each other.

"I have no doubt!" Splash added with a bell's ringing emphasis.

"I've never had cinnamon. Would I like it?" Drip queried, changing the subject, and the conversation that followed grew quite animated as they started their return.

"I'll leave you here," Lacht said when they reached the road to her cottage. "I said good-bye to Curl earlier, when her mother and father carried her into Wasso Lake. She fussed the whole way, but I saw her yawn right before she went under the surface. I only spent one afternoon trapped under that pond, but I'm tired too."

The men insisted on escorting her all the way to her cottage door. She appreciated the courtesy, though she'd rather have walked by herself. Too much had happened. She wanted time alone.

Thankfully, no one in her family had come home yet. She wandered through the rooms, touched familiar things, and snooped in the big front kitchen for leftovers. Half a loaf of homemade bread was in the breadbox, and she cut herself a big piece. Then she smothered her bread with soft butter and ate it, licking her fingers when she'd finished.

Their drinking jar still had water in it, which meant she wouldn't have to go outside to the well. Drinking deeply, she wiped her mouth and yawned.

"I guess I'll lie down," she told herself and stumbled into the bedroom she shared with Irsht.

Kicking off her shoes, she sat on the edge of the bed for several minutes before she could summon up the strength to pull down the covers and slide her legs underneath them. After that feat was accomplished, she yawned again and pulled the covers up to her neck. Then, finally, the need to move ended. Sleep cushioned her gently on all sides, as if it had taken lessons from the golden waters of Wasso Lake.

When she woke the next morning, Lacht felt such a deep sense of comfort that she knew something had happened during the night.

I must have had another dream, she thought; but try as she might, she couldn't remember it clearly. It had something to do with Keshua, which explained the sense of comfort, but she couldn't remember specifics.

"If he wanted me to remember, I would," she said out loud, opening her eyes.

"Have you gone crazy?" Irsht asked, poking her head in the bedroom, "or should I say—crazier?"

"I am a Wet One!" Lacht announced, her nose lifted loftily into the air. "You should speak to me with respect from now on."

"Do Wet Ones bathe?" her little sister asked with a total lack of respect, "because there's hot water in the tub if they do, but I guess you're too important now and no longer need—"

"I'm coming," Lacht said, swinging her feet over the side of the bed. "Is the tub full?"

"Yes, thanks to me," Irsht answered smugly. "I thought even a Wet One might enjoy a hot bath."

"I will have one every morning from now on. See to it," ordered Lacht.

"Ha!" was Irsht's only verbal response as she sprang for her pillow and swung it at her sister.

They hadn't enjoyed a good pillow fight in years. Lacht and Irsht swung and dodged and giggled with the quiet expertise they had once known very well indeed. The quieter they stayed, the longer the fight could last.

"What's going on in there?" the familiar call came at last.

"Nothing," the two sisters chorused and grinned at each other.

"Someone's water is getting cold," sounded an ominous warning.

"No!" Lacht shrieked and dropped her pillow.

"I won!" Irsht crowed, as Lacht grabbed some clothes and dashed from the room.

142

Lacht took a long, leisurely bath and hung lazily around the cottage the rest of the day. The following morning, she made muffins for lunch, then napped three solid hours. The nap revived her. She spent the next few days mapping out a plan for their newly plowed yard and planting a line of blueberry bushes along its sunniest border.

"Mom, where'd you say you wanted a flower bed?" she asked one afternoon, "in shade or sun?"

"Sun," Frenne answered without hesitation. "Pudca's bulbs will bloom better in full sun."

"What are they?" asked Lacht.

She liked flowers.

"Dewbirds and pompas," her mother told her with a pleased smile. "We have dozens of both kinds, and the pompas are mixed colors. I think Pudca wanted to thank your father for visiting her when she was sick."

"Dad's always getting gifts," Lacht remarked absently. "What are dewbirds like?"

"Oh, they're plate-sized flowers that must have reminded whoever named them of birds. I can't say that I see any resemblance, but the leaves do make a pretty blue fringe around the green blooms. They get heavy though. We'll need sticks to prop them up."

"Ploddin will give us sticks," Lacht commented.

She caught the sideways glance her mother gave her but didn't respond to it. Frenne cleared her throat, but Lacht didn't respond to that either, though she knew what was bothering her mother.

Seven days had passed since her return, and she hadn't visited Ploddin once. She'd kept busy and she wasn't avoiding people anymore, but she hadn't visited Ploddin.

"Why don't you ask him? You could go right now," her mother suggested, peering intently out the window and wetting her dishrag. "Oh, look at that green bird's wingspan! Do you think someone named dewbirds after it?"

Lacht rolled her eyes. "You're too obvious, Mom. You shouldn't even try."

"You know, don't you," Frenne said, forgetting green birds that didn't look like flowers and wringing out her dishrag with more energy than necessary, "that Ploddin can't leave his cottage. The Wassandra healer, I forget his name, ordered him not to walk anywhere."

"Blow," Lacht told her. "The healer's name is Blow, and he's a real tyrant from what I hear. Everyone says that he does a good job, though."

"You're changing the subject," her mother scolded.

"No, I'm not," she responded, and her eyes widened innocently. "You mentioned the Wassandra healer."

"All right, why won't you visit Ploddin?" Frenne questioned with a loud sigh as she turned to face her. "I should have known to ask directly in the first place. You and Irsht perfected years ago the technique of avoiding indirect questions."

Lacht stared at the kitchen window. "That window needs cleaning again. Kitchen windows get more spots than any others— which reminds me. I need to scrape smudge off one corner of my bedroom window. It bothers me every night, but when morning comes, I forget all about it."

"Lacht!"

"Yes, sorry," she hastily apologized. "The truth is," and she focused again on the window but didn't really see it this time, "things happened too fast. I thought I liked Crispin in a special way, but when I got to know Ploddin, I liked him too. Those dreams came one after another; my feet stayed dry in Wasso Lake; then Keshua sent me to find Curl.

"Ploddin jumped between us and that monster," she whispered, and her face twisted. "I had to leave him down there. When the pond turned dark, and I thought the Wert had killed him, I realized how much I cared. My feelings for Crispin didn't even come close."

"Is that bad?" her mother asked quietly.

"No, but I've only known him for two, well, three weeks now. It's not long enough, is it?"

Frenne smiled at her.

"It's not long enough to know someone well," she answered honestly, "but it's long enough to make a start. You and Ploddin have had an unusual beginning, that's all."

"Well, my life has left me out of breath," Lacht stated, giving her words several punctuating nods. "I've decided to slow down and think things through like an adult. He hasn't suffered from lack of visitors. Crispin would have taken care of that. Probably, no one has even missed me."

Frenne didn't say anything. She merely began wiping the countertop with her dishrag again.

Lacht watched her. "That's the third time," she finally remarked.

"What?" Frenne asked, startled.

"You've wiped that corner of the counter three times now," Lacht told her. "Wow, it must be really dirty!"

"You're a rascal," her mother said, making a shooing motion in the air. "Why don't you go work on that flowerbed and let me clean my kitchen?"

"Fine," Lacht answered and went outside with a smile and a great show of energy. Once outside though, her smile disappeared.

She'd expected her mother to insist on the visit to Ploddin. Of course, she would have refused to go. However, if her mother had insisted long enough....

Hey, I've made my choice, she reminded herself. *I mean to act like an adult from now on.*

The soil in their yard responded better since Ploddin had plowed it. Her new mattock broke up the remaining dirt clumps with ease. She prepared a large sunny area and smoothed it flat.

An hour later, she put the last dewbird bulb into the ground just as Irsht walked down the road toward home. The two sisters went inside to help with supper.

Roasted fish, scenting the air with the good smells of butter and garlic, stayed warm inside the oven while Frenne fried potatoes, and Irsht tossed a salad. Lacht spooned the applesauce she'd made that morning into a bowl and set it on the table next to the salad.

An abundance of apples grew in the Stalli Mountains. Tart ones, sweet ones, cooking ones, eating ones—some kind of apple was always ripe from mid-summer to late fall; whereas blueberries ripened only for a couple of weeks in late July. Apples stored better than blueberries too, and nobody needed to plant a long line of bushes on the sunny side of the yard in order to enjoy them.

"Apples are as good as blueberries," she commented offhandedly as they sat around the kitchen table, waiting for Winnel to get home.

"Bite your tongue, Lacht," Irsht responded severely. "You shouldn't say things that aren't true."

"By the way," Frenne said, "I found a jar of blueberries that I didn't know I had. Now I can make that girl a pie."

"Oh, Mother, thank you so much," Irsht gushed.

"Not you," Frenne scolded cheerfully. "I meant Curl. She's never tasted blueberry pie, and I promised I'd make her one."

"If she hasn't tasted it, then she won't know what she's missing," argued her younger daughter; "whereas I—"

She didn't get a chance to finish her argument. The door banged open, and Winnel burst into the kitchen as if he'd run all the way from town.

"What happened?" asked Frenne, jumping up and putting a hand over her heart.

"Royalty. I just saw royalty," Winnel announced, panting out the words as he leaned against the kitchen counter and looked at Lacht.

"What?" three voices asked.

146

"The Wassandra healer marched out of the lake ten minutes ago," he told them. "He may not be royalty, but he acts like it. He's going to Ploddin, and I hope the boy is prepared for him. I hope Blow doesn't hurt him this time."

Winnel shook his head from side to side, tightened his lips, and creased his forehead into lines Lacht had never seen on her father's face.

Her hands slammed onto the table, and she erupted out of her chair. "He'd better not!" she said, glaring at her father as if she held him personally responsible for any such behavior on the healer's part.

Then she charged out of the kitchen and down the road.

Winnel watched his daughter go and turned to face the accusing faces of Irsht and Frenne.

"Well," he said, blinking sheepishly. "I thought it might work. What's for supper?"

Fifteen

A Confrontation

L acht confined herself to a fast walk until she came around
the last corner and spotted Crispin standing on the porch,
staring at his own front door. She ran the rest of the way.

"Why are you out here?" she asked as soon as she reached the
edge of the yard.

"Blow doesn't want anyone inside while he's doing his dirty
work," he responded, not moving his gaze from the door.

It was not perhaps the best thing to say.

She marched up the porch steps as if she were royalty herself
and pushed on the door. Someone had locked it.

"Let me in this cottage," she shouted. "Let me in, or you'll
regret it."

The door opened suddenly, and a tall Wassandra man stood in
front of Lacht, looking down his nose at her. His curls were a
darker brown than the other Wassandra's. His eyes were darker
gold too, and the brown glints in them flamed.

"Who is this person?" he questioned, raising his head to stare
at Crispin and completely ignoring Lacht.

Eloquently, the young man shrugged and moved to one side.
He could see better from there.

"I want to come in," Lacht announced, and the Wassandra
healer had to lower his head again and encounter eyes that would
have emitted sparks if they possibly could have.

Silently, they traded fiery glares. Blow turned away first, but he did it with a hint of humor that made Lacht want to growl at him.

"Are Stalli women all this feisty?" he asked Crispin.

"Lacht is one of our best," Crispin assured him solemnly.

Blow looked back at the furious girl before him. "You cannot come in now."

"Why not?" she growled.

"Because my patient is not wearing all his clothes," he informed her. "I do not allow—"

"All right," she hastily agreed, cooling down several degrees, "but I don't want you to hurt Ploddin today. You hurt him badly last time."

"I had to," he announced through his nose.

"You did not," she snapped, "and even if you did, you could have helped by acting like a healer and not a monster."

"Lacht," called a voice from within the cottage, "I'm fine."

"If you hurt him again, you're no better than that Wert," she continued, staring up into the dark gold eyes.

One of Blow's eyebrows lifted. "You are the Stalli girl that went to Curl."

"Yes, and I would like to remind you that Ploddin killed that awful Wert to save—"

"Lacht!" shouted Ploddin, "stop it!"

Tears were coming. They were definitely coming, but Lacht didn't let herself move away. Standing in front of the tall Wassandra man, she stared up at him. The fact that she had to blink several times detracted from the fierce stance she meant to make, but the final results were still gratifying.

"I will take care of him," Blow said with only a slight bit of condescension. "I am a good healer."

"I've heard that," she agreed, "but if you acted nicer, people would feel comforted, and that's part of healing too."

The Wassandra man nodded stiffly, closing the door; and Lacht reached the nearest porch chair two seconds before her legs collapsed.

Grinning, Crispin made fists and started punching the air. She watched him for want of anything else to do. When he'd finished his one-sided, boxing match, he bowed before her.

"That makes two monsters in one week," he whispered.

She had started to respond when a heavy thud sounded from inside the cottage. It seemed a much better idea then to clasp her hands tightly together, and she proceeded to do so; while Crispin stood stiffly, his eyes concentrating on the cottage door once more.

Without warning, the door swung open and Ploddin walked slowly out.

"Ploddin," gasped Lacht. "You're not limping."

"I still have a limp—but it's not nearly as bad," he said in reply, and his face lit up.

"Do not walk more than a few minutes today," Blow instructed his patient, as the healer swept across the porch and down the steps. "Tomorrow, walk a little longer; the next day, longer still; and continue the progression, slowly building up your leg's strength."

"I'll do that, Blow," Ploddin said to the departing, regal back, "and thank you."

They watched the Wassandra man stride majestically down the road toward town. When he finally passed out of sight, they smiled their mutual relief.

"You're better, really?" asked Crispin, as if he couldn't believe it.

"I think so," answered his brother. He sat carefully in the chair next to Lacht.

"I can't believe things turned out this well," Crispin marveled, beaming. "At first, I thought they had you trapped under the water."

"Yes, I heard," Ploddin told him dryly.

The brothers' eyes met.

Crispin nodded once. He cleared his throat and glanced at Lacht, then away again. "Well, I guess I'll see what's going on in town. We have to think of something new to do now that we can't tell scary stories about Wassandra."

He walked out of the yard and down the road. Lacht watched him until he too passed out of sight. Then she studied the unusually tidy yard. Someone had straightened and piled everything. A broom leaned conveniently next to the swept forge.

Meddy must have visited—several times.

"I guess you can go back to work now," she remarked, gazing fixedly at the clean forge.

"I hope so," Ploddin said, staring at the forge along with her. "I got a lot of carving done this week, but I like blacksmithing better."

"Yes, I know," she responded, still not looking at him.

"Lacht—" he began, shifting his body towards her, but she interrupted him.

"Where's Brownie?" she asked in a rush.

"Where do you think? Under the porch, of course."

She ran down the porch steps and peered beneath them. "There you are, Brownie! Oh, I'm so glad to see you. You're a wonderful, dear, sweet dog; do you know that?"

Ploddin made a noise of disgust in his throat, and she sat on the lowest step, grinning. This was better. She was comfortable with this.

"Lacht," he began again, and her grin vanished.

Uh oh.

"You don't need to be afraid of me," was all he said.

She turned sunset pink all over, but she made herself face the young man sitting on the porch above her. He smiled at her. His hair didn't grow as thick and wavy as Crispin's. Crispin had broader shoulders too. Lacht stared at him and didn't care.

If he looked like Crispin, he wouldn't be Ploddin, she thought confusedly.

"Things happened too fast," she said, and he nodded.

"I know, but we can take our time now."

A nose nudged Lacht's hand, and she glanced down at the

small brown dog. She wanted badly to say that Ploddin was every bit as wonderful, dear, and sweet as Brownie, but she could imagine the snort of horror that would follow such a comment.

So she only smiled, but that seemed to satisfy Ploddin. He leaned back in his chair, and they talked, catching each other up on the past week's events.

♫ ♫ ♫

Over the winter, Lacht and Ploddin talked more...much more. Ploddin went back to his metal work, and Lacht learned with remarkably increased interest how to manage a Stalli home. Curl visited Burkin Village as often as her parents would allow, and started a garden.

♫ ♫ ♫

"They're coming up," the Wassandra girl shrieked the following spring when the bulbs she had planted poked small, blue leaves above the ground.

"Of course, they're coming up," Lacht boasted. "I wouldn't hear of anything else."

"I hear things," Curl mentioned, peering slyly through the corners of her eyes at her friend.

"What things?" Lacht asked, leaning down to loosen a dirt clump with her fingers.

"Things about you and Ploddin!" the girl answered, and the brown flecks in her golden eyes hopped sideways.

Lacht smiled at the dirt clump. "Curl, do you ever think of anything besides romance and adventure?" she asked over her shoulder.

"I think about gardening," she answered promptly.

"So you do," Lacht encouraged her, straightening up. "You'll make a good gardener one day."

"Now about you and Ploddin," began Curl who could never be distracted long from romance and adventure.

"We're engaged," Lacht said and winced at the piercing scream that followed her announcement.

"I can't believe you didn't let me see the bread thing," Curl protested indignantly as soon as she had breath.

"The bread thing?" questioned Lacht, though she knew exactly what the girl meant.

"Yes, the asking bread and the answer bread," the Wassandra said with even more indignation. "You know I wanted to see it. It's an old Stalli custom, and I—"

"Some things," interrupted Lacht, "are private, you know. Ploddin came with sweetbread two days ago, and I took him a loaf yesterday, but how on Tarth did you hear about it? You do live under the lake, don't you?"

"I want to come to your wedding," the younger girl begged without answering, sidetracked by the thought of that wonderful event.

"We want you *in* our wedding," Lacht told her. "You will stand next to Irsht."

This time Lacht managed to put a hand over either ear before the scream.

A neighbor walked out on his porch.

"Everything's all right," she called.

The neighbor waved and went back inside.

"We're going to build a new cottage near the lake," Lacht informed the excited girl, "a gray one with gold shutters."

"Ugh!" Curl promptly responded, shaking her head. "Do your shutters have to be gold?"

"Yes," Lacht said firmly, "and you can visit us whenever you want, and we'll visit you too."

"Two Wet Ones marrying," Curl thought out loud. "I bet you'll have Wet One babies."

"We'll see," she answered cheerfully. "I want lots of children,

153

but Ploddin only wants two."

"Two!" Curl responded, her eyes narrowing and lips pursing. "That is just like a man!"

"Lots of men want big families," Lacht said, shaking her head at the girl who obviously considered herself an authority on the subject.

"Look who's coming," Curl screamed, jumping to her feet.

Lacht had not prepared for that one. She rubbed the ringing from her ears as she followed the dancing girl out of the yard and down the road to greet Ploddin and Crispin.

Ploddin walked with a slight limp that would never go completely away. However, his leg no longer ached, keeping him up at night. The cold of winter had set him back some, but with the return of warm weather, he felt better than he could ever remember feeling.

His face brightened at the sight of the girls, and he held out a hand to Lacht, who took it gladly and squeezed it, barely able to keep herself from jumping up and down. Curl's excitement was infectious.

"I'm going to stand beside Irsht in their wedding," Curl told Crispin.

"That's great," he congratulated her heartily and then winked. "If you were a little older, we'd beat them to it, wouldn't we?"

"I'm getting older all the time," she pointed out, batting her eyelashes at him.

Lacht frowned. She didn't want her friend to grow up a flirt— though so far, she had made little headway against the tendency. This afternoon was no different. Curl only smiled in response to Lacht's frown and batted long, dark-gold lashes in her direction.

"Who taught you that?" the older girl asked severely.

"You did," announced Curl roguishly, fluttering her eyelashes again just to show how well she could do it.

"I don't flirt," she protested.

"Well, some girls do," Curl told her, grinning. "When Lynn and Chell visited last fall with their sons, I saw how the Stalli girls

154

acted. If I can't marry Crispin, I'm going to marry Loraf, Mindik, or Chera."

"Now you listen to me," Lacht began a lecture, and it was going to be a lengthy one, but Winnel came out on the porch just then.

"Supper's ready," he called, "and we have cinnamon buns, but you need to hurry because Irsht has already eaten three."

"Dad," his younger daughter scolded from inside the cottage. "I only ate one, but I did it in stages!"

Crispin and Curl sprang to the rescue of the remaining buns, but Ploddin held Lacht back.

"I talked to Crispin today," he whispered as they walked slowly up the porch steps. "He agreed to take all the wood work and give me the metal jobs."

"That will mean a much heavier work schedule for Crispin," she whispered back dryly.

"It'll be good for him," her fiancé admitted. "I should have made him do his share of the work before now. Meddy always said so, but I didn't have the heart. Moving out has made it easier somehow."

"I can't wait until we're living in our own cottage," she said, adjusting her voice back to normal and glancing at her fiancé with happy eyes.

"Down by Wasso Lake," he agreed, smiling at her as he opened the cottage door, "you, me, and two children."

"More than two!" shrieked Curl from the other side of the table.

"Says who?" challenged Ploddin.

He and Lacht walked into the kitchen, the spicy, sweet aroma of cinnamon buns welcoming them.

"ME!"

Three Bear Cinnamon Buns
Randy and Helen Baldwin

Makes a 9x13 pan's worth
(parentheses are my comments—Sally Byrd)

Buns:
5 cups flour
1/8 cup—2 Tablespoons—yeast
1 ½ cup warm water
1 ½ teaspoon salt
2 eggs beaten
1/3 cup oil
3 teaspoons cinnamon—to taste
1/3 cup dark brown sugar
½ cup honey

Filling:
2 cups dark brown sugar
6 Tablespoons cinnamon—
   to taste
1 stick butter
raisins—optional

Icing
1 lb. butter—4 sticks
2 lbs. powdered sugar
4 egg yolks
1 teaspoon vanilla
pecans—optional

Buns: Put flour in bowl and make a hole in the middle, big enough for 1½ cups of warm water. Pour the water in and add the yeast; making a paste out of the water, yeast, and some of the flour. Cover with the rest of the flour, sprinkle salt on top of mound, and let sit in warm place 45 minutes (or longer, fit the timing to your schedule) with dishtowel on top of bowl. (Randy puts his near the heat in a warm bathroom. I put mine in an oven and then preheat the oven for 1 minute to get it warm enough—be sure to turn the oven off again!) As the yeast activates, it should bubble up through the flour like a volcanic eruption! (ours never looked like a full-fledged eruption—just some bubbles—but I love Randy's description and will keep trying!) Add eggs, oil, cinnamon, sugar, and honey. Stir and knead five to ten minutes. Then roll out into a rectangle about an inch thick—it will swell—using flour to keep it from sticking.

<u>Filling:</u> Soften butter and spread on rectangle. Mix together sugar and cinnamon, sprinkle over butter. Spread on top of dough, then roll long side of rectangle together, tucking ends underneath. Cut the rolled dough into pieces about 2 inches thick and place on baking sheet (or 9" by 13" pan). Cover and let rise in warm place an hour or until doubled. Bake 375 degrees until brown, about 15 minutes. Cool.

<u>Icing:</u> Melt butter, then add sugar, egg yolks, and vanilla. Mix well. Spread on cooled buns. May put hot butter on buns first and heat on grill! Very good!

(Note: My daughter, Sarah, and I substituted drained applesauce for the butter in the rolls and filling, and thought the result moist and delicious. My other daughter, Beth, and my son, Stephen, and his wife, Michelle, preferred the butter recipe.)

Don't Miss…

TARTH SERIES
Book One

The Brueggen Stones

S.G. BYRD

Lynn does not panic, Lynn does not scream—
but why is this happening,
and WHEN WILL SHE WAKE UP?

Lynn's an "in-between." Not a child, not an adult—even if she does have a real job in a department store. In fact, her life isn't interesting at all…until the day she trips and bumps her head on a Chicago sidewalk.

Plunged headlong into the world of Tarth and a vicious war between the evil sorcerer, Gefcla, and the kindly Stallis, Lynn decides she should try to fulfill a prophetic rhyme from Keshua, the Healer. Only she can't let anyone else know, or they might try to stop her.

Chell, a Stalli warrior wants to help, but he is hours away—and Gefcla isn't!

Coming Soon...

TARTH SERIES
Book Three

The Opal Cavern

S.G. BYRD

Curl says she'd rather die than spend
the rest of her life trapped under Wasso Lake.
What if her wish is coming true?

Nineteen years old now and still longing to see new things, Curl plans to go on an exploration trip with Lynn's two sons, Mindik and Chera. Their goal is to find Tarth's legendary Opal Cavern, but Lacht has recurrent, heavy feelings that her underwater friend shouldn't go. Nobody, including Lacht, listens to her forebodings until the explorers have left. Then the Wassandra, Wave, learns a secret from an old diary—a secret that can mean life or death for Curl. A rescue team rushes off to find the explorers...but will they be too late?

For more information:
http://otherworlds.wordpress.com
www.oaktara.com

About the Author

Majoring in English and Religion, I graduated from Duke University in 1973. Four years later, I married and had three children, who all grew up reading C.S. Lewis, J.R.R. Tolkien, and George MacDonald. I dreamed of writing stories myself but didn't actually try until my children got older. Over the next ten years, Tarth emerged. *The Brueggen Stones,* the first of four related but separate stories, has already been released.

Under the Golden Mists and its sequel, *The Opal Cavern,* began to form in my imagination when *The Little Mermaid* movie was popular. I started wondering, *If an underwater people lived on Tarth, what would they be like? If an older Lacht and Irsht, the Stalli children from* The Brueggen Stones, *met them, what would happen?*

Other authors have described underwater people in many forms, from fishy to fairy. My Wassandra are not at all fishy; nor are they fairy. They are created beings with souls (unlike the unfortunates in Hans Christian Andersen's tale); however, they are a unique people, golden-skinned, long-fingered, and just as suspicious toward the Stallis who live above them as the Stallis are toward them.

You may write the author at: **SarahGByrd@gmail.com.**

For more information:
http://otherworlds.wordpress.com
www.oaktara.com

Printed in the United States
145647LV00001B/102/P

9 781602 900950